FROZEN SNIPER

DAVID HEALEY

INTRACOASTAL

FROZEN SNIPER

By David Healey

Intracoastal Media digital edition published March 2020. Print edition ISBN 978-0-9674162-4-3

Cover art by Streetlight Graphics

BISAC Subject Headings:

FIC014000 FICTION/Historical

FIC032000 FICTION/War & Military

Ah, brother! only I and thou
Are left of all that circle now—

"Snowbound" by John Greenleaf Whittier

CHAPTER ONE

If Micajah "Caje" Cole had not gone hunting on that perfect fall morning, he never would have found himself, months later, fighting for his life against a Chinese sniper in the frozen Taebaek Mountains of Korea. It was a battle that would come to be known as the Chosin Reservoir, one of the U.S. Army's greatest calamities since ol' Sitting Bull had taught General Custer a thing or two.

But on that crisp fall morning, the future was yet to come, and Cole faced nothing more threatening than coming home empty-handed. Even that wasn't a life-or-death situation. Unlike when he'd been a boy in the shack near Gashey's Creek, when he'd gone to bed hungry on many nights, the larder of Cole's cabin was stocked with canned goods: beans mostly, but also canned peaches and even a few cans of stew and chili.

Cole climbed steadily up the mountain well before daybreak, moving silently in the twilit shadows. He was so quiet that he came upon a fox scratching for mice under a fallen log. The fox didn't sense him until the last moment and then, finally catching sight of Cole, disappeared in a streak of red through the smooth gray trunks of the maples.

Cole grinned. He reckoned that he hadn't lost his touch. His ability to move quietly and unseen had kept him alive through the war. He raised his rifle, a battered but well-oiled Winchester that his old friend Hollis had left him along with the knife-making shop, but changed his mind and let the fox go. No sense wasting a bullet. He wasn't fixin' to eat a fox and it wasn't fur season yet.

He planned to start high on the mountain in the early morning and hunt his way down. It had been the way that his Pa liked to hunt, and he had taught it to Cole. Stalking, you might call it, rather than holing up in a deer blind. The walk was as enjoyable as the hunt. He almost felt as if the old man was rambling alongside him this morning.

Still, Cole's gray eyes caught every flicker of motion in the woods: a squirrel flicking its tail, flitting birds, falling leaves in their bright gold and red. His legs covered the steep ground easily. Cole was a little taller than average, lean and tough as a locust fencepost. He was built for roving the mountains. Dress him in buckskins and give him a flint-lock rifle, and he could have stepped right out of the frontier days.

The sun reached down through the trees and touched his shoulders, warmth spreading through him. Deep, deep inside him, even that primitive part of Cole that he called the Critter and that had also helped keep him alive on the battlefield, finally uncurled itself and relaxed.

* * *

BY NOON, Cole had worked his way down the mountain without seeing much more than a few squirrels, which he wasn't about to waste a shell on and spook any larger game. In a few minutes, he would reach the paved road near the base of the mountain, but he planned to stick to the woods. Since coming home from the war, Cole preferred to keep to himself. He didn't want to meet anyone and spoil the solitude of the morning.

Up ahead, he was surprised to hear voices coming from the direction of the road. Nobody lived along this road deep in the mountains, and traffic was occasional.

He stopped and listened, knowing that sound carried far in the still mountain air. The road was still out of sight, but he could hear a woman's voice, and that of two men. He was still too far away to make out the words, but the tone of fear in the woman's voice was plain enough. Trouble, sure enough. But did he want to make it his trouble? Easiest thing to do was to keep on walking and mind his own business. Deep within him, however, some instinct made the Critter stir. Cole moved closer until he could hear the words plainly.

"Please, leave me alone," said the woman.

"Look at you, out here all by yourself," a male voice said. "Ain't nobody around."

"Scream if you want to," said a different man. He laughed roughly. "There's nobody to hear you."

"No, please don't."

Cole eased through the woods until he could see the road ahead. An old car was pulled to the side of the road, steaming—likely a busted radiator or overheated. Didn't nobody in the mountains have a new car and the steeps parts were rough on old motors.

A pickup truck was nosed in behind the car. He could see a woman backed defensively against the car. Two men stood nearby, pressing in on the woman. Cole was reminded of coyotes circling a wounded deer.

She wore a simple dress and a hand-knit sweater against the autumn chill. The two men looked big—bigger than Cole, anyhow—and one wore a denim jacket and the other had on a heavy leather coat that was too hot for the weather. Both men had longish hair slicked back with hair tonic in that rock 'n roll style that was catching on. Some called it a duck's ass. A man ought not to fool so much with his hair, thought Cole. He fought the urge to grab them by that hair and cut it shorter with the Bowie knife on his belt.

Looking more closely, he saw something familiar about the woman. It took him a few moments to recall the face, back when it was younger and less careworn. He now recognized Norma Jean Elwood, who had stolen his clothes all those years ago when he went swimming in Gashey's Creek, then hooted at him from the bushes as he made his way home naked as a jaybird. It was what passed for flirtation among mountain teenagers.

Cole felt his jaw tighten, along with his grip on the rifle.

"Come on, now," one of the men was saying. "We'll give *you* a ride if you give *us* a ride. And we don't mean in a car."

"Ya'll can go to hell," Norma Jean said.

The men circled closer, boxing her in.

Cole stepped from the woods onto the hard macadam road.

Both men spun, startled. Cole had come out of nowhere. The young woman's face showed relief, but not recognition. That day on Gashey's Creek had been a long time ago.

"You boys run along now," Cole said. He held the rifle balanced in the crook of his left elbow, not pointing at the men.

"Best mind your own damn business," said the one in the leather coat, ignoring Norma Jean as he focused on Cole, his initial surprise giving way to anger.

The other man just glared.

Cole held his ground. "It's a hell of a thing, seeing two men like you bothering this woman, when you ought to be helping her."

"Like I said, mind your own business unless you want to get hurt."

"I reckon I done decided to make this my business," Cole said. "And I ain't the one that's gonna get hurt."

A car came by, the first one yet, slowed down at the sight of four people standing in the road, then the driver seemed to sense the trouble that was coming and sped up, racing off toward town.

"The sheriff will be coming now," Norma Jean said.

The two men looked at each other, and Cole could almost see the message flash between them. Even if the sheriff was coming, it would take him another twenty minutes to get here—and that's if he happened to be in town and not clear on the other side of the county. In the meantime, they reckoned that two against one was good odds.

The fact that these two didn't seem trouble at the sight of Cole's rifle made him realize that at least one them was armed. He took the rifle in two hands now and leveled it at the man in the leather coat, who had started to move, reaching for something under that heavy coat.

"Don't," Cole said.

Grinning, the man ignored him. The man's hand reappeared with a pistol in it.

Cole shot him through the heart.

The second man in the denim jacket went running for the pickup truck. Cole was happy to let him go. He levered another shell into the chamber, but stupidly, he lowered the rifle. He'd lost his edge since the war.

Instead of jumping into the truck and driving off, which is what anybody with a lick of sense would have done, the second man grabbed something from under the seat and came running at Cole. Nearly too late, Cole spotted the sawed-off shotgun. He just had time to step in front of Norma Jean before the man fired.

Lucky for Cole, the man had been in too much of a hurry to aim— as much as you even had to aim a short-barreled shotgun loaded with buck and ball. Part of the blast plucked at Cole's sleeve and the rest hit the front of Norma Jean's car, shattering the headlamp. Glass showered down on the road with a tinkling sound that trailed the shotgun blast.

"Shit!" the man shouted.

Cole didn't give him a chance to empty the other barrel, but fired from his hip like an Old West rifleman. Cole's bullet caught him square in the chest. The man flew back against the open door of the pickup truck and then slid down into the roadside weeds. *Lucky shot*, Cole thought, a bit impressed with himself. Not so lucky for the dead man.

He turned to the woman. "You all right?" he asked.

"Damn them," she said. "Look what those two gone and made you do."

To Cole's surprise, Norma Jean was not breaking down into hysterics, but had a grim set to her face as she studied the grisly scene.

"I didn't mean to kill them," Cole said. He knew that sounded foolish, looking at the two dead men, but instinct had kicked in as if the rifle had a mind of its own.

"You sure did a good job of shooting them dead for someone who didn't mean to," Norma Jean said, matter-of-factly. "But if ever two men needed killing, it was them two. If I'd had a gun, I would of done it myself. You won't catch me without one again, let me tell you."

Cole raised an eyebrow. Stated in her matter-of-fact tone, it did not sound like boasting.

He looked around at the scene they were now in the middle of. The beautiful fall morning had gone to hell in a handbasket. Without a breeze, a tang of gunpowder hung in the air. A trickle of blood ran down the road from under the man in the leather coat, from where his heart had pumped it out. If someone hadn't known better, it would have almost looked like water spilled onto the road.

The dead man's pistol lay nearby. Cole wasn't surprised to see that it was an Army-issue Browning 1911—a lot of those had made it home from the war, although he doubted that these two had actually been soldiers.

They heard the noise of a motor approaching and both looked in that direction. A lumber truck rolled to a stop, seeing the trouble.

"You best be gone before the sheriff shows up," Norma Jean said. "Those two had it comin', but the sheriff might not see it that way."

Cole nodded, but he couldn't yet bring himself to disappear into the woods. "I reckon you don't remember me," he said. "I'm—

"I know who you are," she interrupted him. "You're that Cole boy I used to know, come back from the war a hero. But I ain't goin' to tell the sheriff I seen you, now am I?"

"Thank you."

"Go on now, before that truck driver gets a look at you," she said.

Cole took one last glimpse of the two bodies on the road. They lay in the shapeless way of the dead that he knew all too well. He had thought he was done with killing.

Then he nodded at Norma Jean and slipped into the mountain forest. In the distance, he could hear the wail of a police siren, rising and falling, almost like a hunting dog chasing its quarry. Coming after him. Maybe Norma Jean would either tell the sheriff what he'd done, or she wouldn't, but either way, Cole had a feeling that everything was about to change.

CHAPTER TWO

COLE HIKED the six miles from the paved road to his cabin, keeping to the woods, staying out of sight. But for all he knew, the law might already be waiting for him there.

His cabin stood halfway up the slope of the mountain behind Hollis' place. The knife-maker's widow had offered to let him live on the second floor of the barn over the knife shop or build on some level pastureland nearby, but Cole preferred his privacy. The only reason that the cabin wasn't all the way up the mountain was that the land grew too steep and getting materials any higher up was too challenging.

As it was, a narrow and hazardous dirt road struggled to reach his cabin—more trail than road, really, and nothing that someone would travel by accident. Potholes the size of buckets and steep drop-offs dissuaded any visitors, which was just fine with Cole. He had added a "Keep Out" sign at the bottom of the hill to emphasize the point. The difficulty of driving the road didn't matter much to him, considering that he had not gotten around yet to buying a vehicle. No Cole in the far reaches of history had owned more than a horse or mule, but he supposed he wouldn't mind driving somewhere from time to time.

He had built the one-room cabin himself, hammering it together out of rough-cut lumber and roofing it with sheets of corrugated metal.

He had taken extra care with that roof, making sure that it didn't leak, and sealing any nail holes with hot pitch. No electricity, no plumbing. He had dug a hole and built an outhouse over it. Though new, the cabin wasn't much different from something straight out of the 19th century. The solitude and simplicity of the cabin suited Cole just fine.

He stoked the fire in the tin potbelly stove and heated a can of store-bought chili—his hunt that morning hadn't been all that success-ful. He was just finishing the last bite when he heard a motor, way down at the bottom of the hill.

"Goddammit," he muttered.

Cole didn't know if it was trouble coming or not, but it was good to be prepared. He had two guns in the cabin, the rifle and a 12-gauge shotgun. Cole opted for the double-barreled Iver Johnson shotgun. Though battered and worn, every inch of the well-oiled metal gleamed. He loaded the shotgun with double-ought shells and stuck several more shells in his coat pocket, where he could reach them in a hurry. He hooked the shotgun in the crook of his left elbow, the breech open. Keeping the gun open would send a message that he was willing to talk. Snapping the gun shut would mean that the conversation was over.

He went out and stood on the front porch of the cabin, waiting. Slowly, laboriously, the Ford car wound its way up the mountain, head-lights cutting into the deepening shadows. He could see that it was the county sheriff.

A deputy was driving, with the sheriff beside him. Cole had met Sheriff Bill Johnson a few times and knew him to be a man who ladled out the law fairly. In this county, sheriff was an elected position that required combining one-part law enforcement and two-parts of good ol' boy politician. He was like a walking, talking recipe for a moonshine cocktail.

After struggling up the rough road, the car came to a stop with what seemed to be a sense of relief. The deputy switched off the engine and got out, but stayed there, keeping the vehicle between him and Cole. Cole didn't recognize the deputy, but he didn't like the man standing where he couldn't see what he was up to.

Sheriff Johnson didn't wear a coat, so that his uniform and badge were plain to see. He was a big man, squarely built, with a belly that hung just a bit over his wide leather belt with its big shiny buckle. No holster on his hip. The sheriff got out and stretched.

"Mr. Cole, that is one hell of a road," he said. "In fact, it's more like a Billy goat path."

"Keeps the traffic down," Cole said, keeping to the shadows on the porch.

"I'm sure it does," the sheriff said. He advanced cautiously now, seeing that Cole held a shotgun. It wasn't an unusual greeting in the mountains, where folks tended toward suspicion. "We just come up here to talk."

On the other side of the big Ford, the deputy shifted and banged a rifle down across the hood.

Cole snapped the shotgun closed and leveled it at the lawmen. *Conversation over.*

There was nothing quite like the muzzle of a double-barreled shotgun to stop a man in his tracks. Sheriff Johnson froze. It would be an even bet whether his puckered sphincter was darker than the muzzle of that shotgun. He then turned to see what his deputy was doing to provoke Cole, saw the deputy leaning across the hood with a rifle, and shouted, "Cole, now don't you shoot! Barney, put down that rifle, goddammit. You want to get us both killed? Come out from around the car."

"But sheriff, he's got a shotgun—"

"Do it!" the sheriff ordered. Holding out his hands to show that they were empty, he turned his attention back to the porch, and although he addressed the deputy, the words were meant for Cole. "Cole here is a war hero. Show him some respect. Let's get this sorted out."

"But sheriff, he shot two men—"

"Shut up, Barney," the sheriff said, not making much effort to disguise his annoyance with the deputy. "Like I said, let's get this sorted out. Cole's not gonna shoot us. Are you, Cole?"

"I reckon not," Cole said. He snapped the shotgun open and stepped down off the porch to meet the sheriff halfway.

The sheriff kept his hands raised, not quite up in the air like he was surrendering, but to show that he wasn't any threat. Beside him, the deputy eyed Cole warily.

"Real nice place you got here," the sheriff said, saying it like he meant it. He looked around and seemed to admire the trees and the mountain stillness. He took a deep breath of the clean air and sighed. "Beats living in town, that's for damn sure."

"Built it myself," Cole said. His voice felt rusty and he realized that whole days went by when he didn't speak to a single person. Between talking to Norman Jean this morning and now the sheriff, he felt like a politician going around making stump speeches.

"That's good. A man ought to build himself a house with his own two hands. Not enough of that these days. That's how our people did it, back in the old days." The sheriff put his hands on his hips, as if signaling that he was getting down to business. "I suppose you know what this is about."

Cole didn't say anything.

The deputy spoke up: "See, Sheriff, I done told you—"

"Let me handle this, Barney," the sheriff said, cutting him off. "Cole, there's two men dead down on the road into town. Would you know anything about that?"

Still, Cole kept quiet.

The sheriff sighed and hitched up his pants. The deputy was fidgeting, but the sheriff seemed used to mountain people like Cole who didn't say much. He took his time filling the silence before he said, "I asked myself, who around here could gun down two men like that and then slip off into the woods like a ghost? Had to be a hunter. Maybe even somebody who had been a soldier."

"Lots of men around here was in the war," Cole said.

"You mean like Deputy Gibson?" the sheriff said, nodding to indicate his deputy. "What did you do in the war, Barney?"

The deputy hesitated. "Fixed broken Jeeps, mostly. I never made it overseas."

"Everybody done his part that was in uniform," Cole said. "Ain't no shame in that."

"Yeah, well, some done more than others," the sheriff said. "Like you, for instance. For what it's worth, the woman didn't tell me a thing, other than that whoever came along saved her from those men. Tight-lipped, yessir. Now, the truck driver said he saw a man with a rifle who stepped off into the woods. I got to thinking about who around here could shoot two men through the heart and I have to say that you came to mind."

"Fair enough."

"Those two were a known quantity around here. They styled them-selves as outlaws, I guess you'd say. Always looking for trouble. They figured themselves as hard men. They didn't know what they'd run into, now did they?"

"Let's take him in, sheriff," the deputy said.

"Shut up, Barney," the sheriff said. He paused. "What Deputy Gibson means is that we'd be obliged if you came with us into town so we can settle some questions about this shooting business."

"Are you arresting me?"

"No need for that," the sheriff said. "Let's just go into town and clear this up."

"All right," Cole said. "I'll need a few minutes to close up."

"Take your time," the sheriff said. "It wouldn't be honest of me not to say that you might be gone a while."

Cole nodded and turned back toward the cabin, but not before he heard the deputy mutter, "Yeah, he might be gone twenty years to life."

The sheriff hadn't come out and said that, but Cole knew that the deputy had it right. Should he go into town with them? Cole didn't see how he had any other options. He had shot those men, even if they'd had it coming. But this wasn't like the war. You couldn't just shoot somebody—two somebodies, he reminded himself—and not expect to bring down the law on your head.

He had half a mind to disappear for good into the woods. But he didn't really want to be a fugitive for the rest of his days. Maybe the sheriff was right, and this could be cleared up one way or another. It was the only chance Cole could see of getting out of this mess.

He walked into the cabin. Looking back into the clearing through the one window, he could see the two lawmen watching the cabin. The sheriff had more of a hangdog expression on his face, as if he'd rather be doing something else, but the deputy looked eager.

"You want me to go around back in case he makes a run for it?" the deputy asked, loud enough for Cole to hear.

"No, you stay put. We've had enough people shot in this county for one day."

"I won't shoot him if I don't have to."

"Cole ain't the one I'm worried about gettin' shot."

Cole unloaded the shotgun, stowed the shells with the others in a box high on a shelf above the door, and took an extra minute to wrap the shotgun in an oily rag. He did the same with his rifle. Then he hid both guns under a loose floorboard beneath his cot. It was the best he could do in a short amount of time, and like the sheriff had said, he might be awhile. The stove was already out.

He walked out and pulled the door shut. There wasn't any lock.

"You are doing the right thing, Mr. Cole," the sheriff said. "You ride up front with me."

The deputy wasn't pleased. "Why do I have to ride in back like a criminal?"

"Because Mr. Cole here ain't a criminal, neither. And to be honest, I prefer Mr. Cole as a conversationalist."

"Sheriff, he ain't said a dozen words."

"Exactly," the sheriff said. "Barney, you are finally catching on."

THEY DROVE DOWN THE MOUNTAIN, just ahead of nightfall, which was just as well because the narrow dirt track would have been treacherous to navigate in the dark. Once they reached the highway, they drove past the spot where the shooting had taken place. A couple of state police cars were out there now, along with a man with a camera who appeared to be a reporter. The sheriff didn't slow down or comment on the scene.

When they reached town, they drove directly to the sheriff's office next to the courthouse. Although there were spaces in front on the street, the sheriff parked in back, then led the way into the office. It wasn't a big space, just a couple of desks, a cramped office for the sheriff, and two cells. Cole didn't like the looks of those bars.

"Have a seat, Mr. Cole. You want some coffee?"

"Thank you, but I'm fine."

"All right. I'm going to call across the street and try to catch the judge."

"The judge? Do you reckon I need a lawyer?"

"Maybe, but let's see what the judge has to say first."

"If you say so." Cole wasn't in any hurry to get a lawyer, anyhow. He trusted them about as much as your average rattlesnake.

The sheriff left a message with the judge's clerk and hung up. They didn't have to wait long. The sheriff's phone rang, and he disappeared into his office to answer it. He returned a minute later and nodded at Cole. "Let's take a walk over to the courthouse and talk to Judge Dorsey."

Leaving the deputy behind, they crossed the street and entered the stately brick courthouse. Cole realized he still wasn't wearing hand-cuffs, which he took to be a good sign.

It was late in the day, so most people had gone home. Their foot-steps rang in the empty courthouse halls. The judge's chambers were on the first floor. Cole followed the sheriff and found himself in what looked like a small library, filled floor to ceiling with leather-bound law books. The place had a good smell of old leather and cigars, with an underlying hint of bourbon. They had entered using a door on the hallway, but another door in the office itself opened up into the empty courtroom. Behind a large wooden desk sat a small, white-haired man with blazing, coal-black eyes. Those were the eyes of every sawmill foreman and banker that Cole had ever seen. Cole's heart sank.

The sheriff started to explain the situation, but Judge Dorsey waved him off. "I know all about it. Sounds like those two got what they deserved. It's likely that their demise saved the taxpayers some money and trouble. Anyhow, I know all about you, Mr. Cole. You are a goddamn war hero. But the thing is, we can't have you goin' around shootin' people. So the sheriff and I have come to a solution."

"Does it involve jail?"

"Not if we can help it, Mr. Cole. With the war in Korea, there's been a recruiting drive," the sheriff explained. "There's a bus leaving in the morning, taking recruits to basic training. It would be best if you're on that bus."

Cole could not believe what he was hearing. "I'm done with the Army."

"But maybe the Army ain't done with you," Judge Dorsey said. His black eyes glittered. "Besides, the Army sure as hell beats prison."

"A lot of veterans are re-enlisting," the sheriff went on in a reasonable tone. "It's a chance for you to be a hero again rather than get dragged through the mud with some sort of trial. The prosecutor we've got now doesn't see things quite the way that the judge and I do, so there's no telling what he's apt to pull. He's just not what you'd call sensible. He wants to make a name for himself and run for judge."

The judge snapped those glittering black eyes at the sheriff, as if he had said too much.

Now, Cole started to understand. The judge and the sheriff didn't want the prosecutor to have any kind of case that might threaten the judge's re-election, and maybe the sheriff's, too. If Cole was on the other side of the world, he'd be safely out of reach.

"If this goes to trial, you might need to hire yourself a real lawyer, not a court-appointed one. No offense, Mr. Cole, but it don't seem like you got the money for that."

"The sheriff and I figured this would be a good way to avoid any trouble for you with this shooting business," Judge Dorsey added. "The last thing we want to see is you arrested. But this needs to cool off. By the time you get back, nobody is going to remember those two fools you shot, or much care. You'll be a war hero all over again."

Cole felt like he was being railroaded, but the judge and the sheriff had a point. If it went to trial, he didn't have the money for a good lawyer. Finally, he nodded in agreement.

"All right, it's decided," the sheriff said. "We'll head back across the street to my office. You'll have to sleep in one of the cells, but the cell won't be locked. Bus leaves in the mornin'."

CHAPTER THREE

THE NEXT DAY, Cole found himself getting off a bus at boot camp. He would have been happier, if happier was the right word, going directly to the front. But the army had determined that he needed training all over again in how to be a soldier—and how to shoot and kill people, which was ironic, considering that he had ended up in this situation by doing just that.

Cole was feeling sullen as a kicked dog. He vowed that he wasn't going to do anything to stand out, or even to be much of a soldier. With any luck, this whole business in Korea would get settled long before he was shipped out. He might even get home to his cabin and beloved mountains after a few weeks or months, once things had settled down.

He looked around the compound, which was surrounded by a chain-link fence, at the neatly ordered rows of Quonset huts and the worn parade grounds. One good thing, he thought, was that they were going into the cooler weeks. Those Quonset huts would be like bake ovens in the summer heat. In the winter, it would be cold as a church on Monday.

Lost in his own thoughts, he hardly noticed the kid next to him until he spoke up.

"I think I made a mistake," the kid said in a squeaky voice. The kid wore glasses that were starting to slide down his nose, and he used a finger to push them back into place. "What was I thinking, signing up?"

"That would be a normal reaction," Cole agreed. "It's kind of like waking up with a hangover and a fat lady next to you."

That image prompted a half-smile. "My name's Tommy Wilson, by the way."

"Cole," he responded. "Listen, kid, this ain't my first rodeo. Just keep your head down and do what the sergeant says."

"If you say so," Tommy said. "Hey, why did you sign up if you knew what you were in for?"

"It was this or go to prison," Cole said.

The kid opened his mouth as if to ask another question, but at that moment, the drill sergeant appeared. He was no more than five-foot-six, but muscles bulged in his neck and he had a way of walking that made him resemble an oncoming locomotive, complete with steam coming out of his ears.

"All right, you maggots, shut your traps!" he shouted. "You don't talk again until I tell you to talk. Is that clear?"

Startled, the busload of new recruits fell silent. But the drill instructor wanted an answer. He must have seen Cole talking earlier, because he squared off against him and shouted into his face: "Is that clear?"

Cole stood at attention and shouted back, "Yes, Sergeant!"

The drill instructor nodded, jaw muscles working as he sized Cole up. Cole stared at a point somewhere above the sergeant's head. "What's your name?" the man demanded.

"Cole, Sergeant."

"Cole, have you done this before?"

"Yes, Sergeant."

The sergeant shook his head as if disappointed. "Goddammit, Cole! Who is stupid enough to rejoin the army?"

When Cole didn't answer right away, the kid standing next to him felt compelled to say, "He said it was prison or the army."

The drill instructor didn't even look at the kid, but kept his eyes boring into Cole. "Is that right? Huh. I am going to keep an extra eye on you, Cole. Understood?"

"Yes, Sergeant!"

After another moment of fierce staring that indicated the sergeant would like nothing better than to bore a hole through Cole with his eyes, the sergeant moved on to shout at other recruits that he didn't like the looks of.

And so it begins, Cole thought.

Cole wished that he had kept his mouth shut instead of jawing with the kid. That damn kid had spilled the beans about the army or prison, putting him square in the sergeant's sights. He'd be keeping to himself from now on. He also realized that his own plan to keep his head down had already gone out the window.

* * *

THE NEW RECRUITS, including Cole, were subjected to physicals that left no part unprobed. What any of that poking and prodding had to do with being fit to carry a weapon, he still hadn't figured out from the last war, other than that the whole procedure was intended to remind the recruits that they were no better than cattle being inspected at a livestock auction.

They lined up for shots against tropical diseases, and then they all got buzzcuts. Cole's hair had not been long to begin with, but he was left with nothing more than some bristle on his head. He'd done this before, back in boot camp a few years ago, but that didn't mean he liked being herded around like cattle.

Finally, they received their new uniforms. There were no mirrors, but Cole didn't need one because all that he had to do was look around: he was sure that he looked pretty much like every other guy there, if a little older: bald, confused, and wearing a brand-new army uniform.

For Cole, who had done it all before, boot camp was simply some-thing to be endured. While it wasn't exactly a pleasant experience to repeat, he also knew that a man generally survived boot camp. It was only after you got out of boot camp that you really had to worry.

One thing that didn't bother Cole was the food, which was plentiful and hearty. He even kind of liked the creamed chipped beef on toast that was served for breakfast—nicknamed SOS or shit on a shingle by some.

The first few days passed in a blur of pushups, calisthenics, and long runs wearing boots. Cole didn't mind so much because he was in good shape from his treks through the mountains. He was glad again that he had given up cigarettes and stayed away from liquor. The more out-of-shape recruits, especially the smokers among them, paid a heavy price those first few days.

Among those who struggled was the kid who had gotten Cole called out on arrival at boot camp. Mainly, the kid seemed to lack confidence in himself that he could do what he was asked. The others ignored him or were caught up in their own suffering as they ran. But Cole knew from experience that if one person in the squad faltered, it would hold them all back. Especially once they made it to Korea. This was all part of learning teamwork.

Cole slowed his pace and dropped back until he was running beside the kid.

"I can't do this," Tommy Wilson muttered. Each of his steps was sloppy and unsteady, eating up even more of what little energy he had.

"I reckon you can," Cole said quietly. "You just don't know it yet. Pick up your feet like you mean it. Lift those knees. You got to use your leg muscles—those are some of the strongest muscles—even on you."

"Gee, thanks."

"Go on now," Cole said. "Make those legs work."

"You ought to leave me."

"Not a chance of that," Cole said. "Now, are you gonna run or does the sergeant need to put a boot up your ass?"

It was hard to say whether the kid was inspired by Cole or just afraid of the sergeant; in either case, he started to run instead of stumble along, pumping his arms and lifting his legs.

"Happy now?" Tommy gasped.

"You're getting the hang of it," Cole said.

Cole's actions did not go unnoticed. They were back at camp, done with the run, everyone doubled over and gasping for air, when the drill instructor took him aside. The sergeant, tough and compact, had run along with the group, and he didn't even seem winded.

"Are you trying to do my job for me, Cole?" the sergeant asked quietly.

Cole snapped to attention. "No, sir!"

A hint of a smile played across the sergeant's leathery face. "I finally got ahold of your file, Cole. You're quite the war hero. One hell of a shot, from what I understand. I can't wait to see you out on the range."

"That was a while ago, sir."

"Yeah? We'll see about that. We can use some snipers in Korea. It turns out that the Chinese are shooting the hell out of our boys."

"Yes, sir."

Cole was relieved when the sergeant moved off to shout at some men who had the audacity to sit on the ground.

The truth was, he was not looking forward to the rifle range. He was determined to serve his time in the army by keeping his head down, and then get back home in one piece. He didn't see how fighting the North Koreans and the Chinese was America's fight. It definitely wasn't his fight. Anyhow, he was done with being a sniper. He didn't want to be in the Army and he didn't want to be in this war, so in his own stubborn way, he had made up his mind not to give the army use of his best skills. With any luck, he would find himself assigned to the motor pool, fueling up tanks and trucks and Jeeps. Hell, he'd be glad to be assigned to a kitchen, even if it meant peeling potatoes all day. Cole's days as a sniper were over.

Finally, they were issued their rifles. The weapon of choice for the U.S. Army remained the M-1. This was the rifle that could be credited in many ways with winning the Second World War. Cole's weapon had been the bolt-action Springfield. Nowadays, this was strictly a sniper weapon, although some M-1 models had been adapted as sniper rifles.

"This rifle is your new best friend," the drill instructor informed them. "You will learn to field strip this weapon and reassemble it like you would brush your teeth. Then and only then, will you learn to properly fire this weapon."

Long before they were given any live ammo, they were drilled in the operation and maintenance of the weapon. While Cole had been known for possibly having the cleanest rifle in Europe, he also knew that these rifles were real workhorses and highly forgiving. They tended to function no matter how much abuse was thrown at them, which made the M-1 a solid military weapon. Short of packing the action or the barrel with mud, the damn thing would still shoot straight.

But the Army had its way of doing things, and that included endlessly cleaning the M-1. Once again, the kid who had lagged behind in his running also had trouble stripping his rifle and putting it back together again. No surprise there.

Cole watched him struggle for a while, desperately practicing in the few minutes before lights out, then sat down next to him on the footlocker.

"It ain't a wrestling match," Cole said. "This rifle was made to come apart, and fit back together, smooth as can be."

"If you say so."

"Don't believe me, huh? Try it again."

This time, Cole put his hands over top of Tommy's, guiding him through the disassembly and assembly, starting by swinging the trigger guard forward, unlocking the action so that it could be removed from the stock. They moved on to removing the spring. Once they were finished, Cole had him run through it again. And again.

Now, the kid was grinning. "I got it!"

"Better," Cole agreed. "All it takes is practice. Now, do it again."

The kid gave him a look. "You got me through that run the other day, and now this. Why are you helping me?"

"I'm not just helping you, kid. I'm helping us all. Who gets the blame when one of us screws up? We all do, right?"

"Well, thanks, anyhow. You saved my bacon."

"Like I said, we're all part of the same pig, kid."

Finally, the day came for the rifle range. Most of the men were excited about getting to shoot live ammunition after days spent merely cleaning or drilling with their rifles.

Cole wasn't as eager. He knew that the drill instructor expected a lot out of him and would be watching him closely. The sergeant wasn't the only one. A handful of other sergeants and non-coms had gathered to see the show. Apparently, word had gotten out that Caje Cole, one of the deadliest U.S. snipers of the previous war, had returned to the range.

The sergeant went through the instructions. It made Cole more than a little nervous that he put so much emphasis on keeping the rifles pointed down range. The last thing that Cole wanted was to get shot in boot camp. He looked around for the kid and hoped that he was listening. If anyone was going to forget his muzzle discipline, it was that one.

Cole mused that around the world, Americans had this reputation as all being gunslingers—either cowboys or gangsters or maybe even pioneer holdouts from the days of Daniel Boone. Sure, there were a few like that—Cole included. But he recalled that his old spotter and fellow sniper, Vaccaro, hadn't done any shooting other than at the carnival games at Coney Island. Vaccaro had caught on eventually and become a passable shot, but he was probably more typical of the average American. The legends about Americans being crack shots and expert riflemen were just that—legends.

The presence of the sergeant nearby pulled Cole out of his reverie. He nodded at Cole and said, "I've been looking forward to seeing what you got. I expect to see some real shooting out there today."

"Yes, sir."

In squads, the soldiers approached the firing line. Their first position would be prone, possibly because it was harder for a man to wave his rifle around and accidentally shoot something when he was lying on the ground. Some of the more enterprising men had stuffed cotton into their ears of their own accord—the army hadn't gotten around to worrying about hearing protection. The targets themselves were rectangular, roughly the size of a man's torso, and covered with a bulls-eye. At this range, the targets were the army's equivalent of hitting the broad side of a barn, but he was sure that some of the men in his squad would find the targets challenging, nonetheless.

Cole took his position. A flag fluttered downrange, signaling that the range was in use. The fabric also gave Cole an indication of which way the wind was blowing, so that he could adjust his shooting.

He followed the sergeant's commands, barely listening. He sure as hell didn't need someone to tell him how to shoot. The stock fit perfectly against his shoulder and against his cheek. These were open sights, not a telescope, but the targets were close enough. Cole breathed deeply, enjoying the autumn sun on his face and the smell of gun oil on the warm, gleaming metal of the rifle barrel. Around him, the other men began to fire.

Dimly, he was aware that the sergeant had come to stand just behind him.

Cole's finger began to take up tension on the trigger.

For Cole, the target had an almost gravitational pull. His bullets wanted to find that target in the same way that the moon circled the earth or the earth circled the sun.

But he reminded himself that he needed to keep his head down. Stubbornly, he had decided that he wasn't going to play the army's game. Cole the sniper was in the past. Wasn't he?

The rifle bucked against his shoulder, not that the M-1 had a bad kick. The rifle's gas system lessened the recoil compared to Cole's old Springfield.

Cole fired five carefully placed shots.

Behind him, the sergeant grunted. "I've got to say, that's goddamn disappointing."

At this distance, it was easy enough to see that not one of Cole's shots had hit the target.

"I reckon I've lost my touch, sir," Cole said.

"Goddammit, Cole, that's not all you've lost. You lost me a fifty-dollar bet with the other sergeants that you would hit the bullseye."

After Cole's performance on the range, which did not improve, the drill sergeant no longer seemed interested in Cole, who did what he was told and worked hard not to stand out. In fact, the only time that the sergeant paid Cole the slightest attention was one day when he cut through the kitchen where Cole was on KP duty, paring knife in one hand and potato in the other.

"Better get used to it," the sergeant said ruefully. "That might just be all that you're good for in Korea if you can't shoot straight."

Cole tossed a freshly peeled potato into the pot and said, "I reckon that's just fine by me, sir."

CHAPTER FOUR

COLE MIGHT HAVE SPENT the next few weeks on extra KP duty, but he got a reprieve. Just days later, Cole's unit shipped out for Korea. Never mind the fact that they weren't fully trained or prepared. Nobody much cared about that. There was a war on. Korea was being overrun, and the U.S. Army needed boots on the ground as soon as possible.

He found himself on a troop train to the West Coast, and then on a ship. Cole had never seen the Pacific Ocean, but a glimpse of the rolling swells was enough for him before he went below. Aside from the occasional visit to a swimming hole as a boy, he never had much liked the water in any way, shape or form. He much preferred two feet on dry ground.

A troop ship was hardly what you might call luxury travel. Too many men were crammed into too little space. The air below decks smelled of diesel fumes and damp metal, armpits and dirty laundry. The sooner that they got where they were going, the better.

Cole knew little of Korea's proud history, let alone any of the politics involved, but understood that the soldiers could probably expect a fight once they got there.

* * *

ACCORDING TO LEGEND, Korea was founded by the god-king Dangun more than two millennia ago, in roughly the epoch in which Christ was born on a distant continent. Wise and resourceful, Dangun ruled for more than a thousand years as the people of Korea flourished, largely in peace.

By the twentieth century, however, Korea's fortunes had fallen. Koreans suffered under Imperial Japan, whose wealthy hunters and landowners saw Korea as little more than a backwards rural fiefdom to be exploited. The arrival of the Second World War meant yet more suffering for the Koreans under Japanese occupation. To the north lay China, a nation that could have been a more powerful ally but that had paid a steep price for not keeping pace with the development of the modern world. China had become embroiled in its own Civil War with the Communists eventually ascending.

In hopes of preventing Korea from falling under the sway of the Communists, the United States had propped up a puppet democracy under a political strongman named Syngman Rhee. Those who had opposed the corruption and brutality under Rhee had sometimes welcomed the Communists at first, as a liberating force. They had soon learned the hard way that the cruelty of the Communists made Rhee's government look like a bunch of petulant Boy Scouts by comparison. The Communists imposed death squads, imprisoned anyone who was somewhat educated, and starved the rest of the population into submission.

For the average Korean, especially those in rural areas, it probably mattered very little who ruled, so long as there was peace in the land. Alas, it was the everyday Korean people who would largely suffer as war swept the peninsula.

* * *

BEFORE THEIR SHIP LEFT PORT, the troops aboard had received one last mail call. Cole was surprised to hear his name. Who the hell was writing to him? Nobody in his family was the letter-writing type. He tucked the envelope away in a pocket, barely even glancing at the handwriting.

Meanwhile, the voyage was long and dull. Soldiers played cards or read battered paperback Westerns and detective stories. Mostly, Cole kept apart from the others. He stayed below and slept, not being particularly eager to gaze out at endless miles of rolling waves.

One distraction came when he found an amateur artist in the ranks who had managed to bring along a little paint and some brushes. Cole paid him a few dollars to paint a Confederate flag on his helmet, similar to the one that had decorated his helmet as he had fought his way across Europe.

"I hate to tell you this, buddy," the artist had said, smiling with satisfaction as he inspected his own work. "But you do know that the South lost the war, right? You sure you want that Johnny Reb flag on your helmet?"

"It's for good luck," Cole explained.

The artist raised his eyebrows. "Geez, I'd hate to see your idea of *bad* luck."

From time to time, Cole took out the letter that he had received and considered opening it. But why embarrass himself? He couldn't read it. Hell, he couldn't even puzzle out the return address to see who had sent it. Clearly, it was someone who didn't know him all that well, or they wouldn't have bothered to write him a letter. Growing up a poor mountain boy, Cole never had gotten around to learning his letters. Poor but proud, Cole's only real source of embarrassment in this world was that even a child could read better than him.

But finally, even Cole couldn't stand the curiosity. Maybe the boredom of the voyage was getting to him. He wanted to know what was in that letter.

Cole had gotten friendly enough with the kid from boot camp, who had a bunk not far away. Tommy Wilson had kept his head down during basic, doing what he was told the best that he could and keeping his mouth shut. At the same time, the kid kept his eyes open, watching and learning. Cole found these to be admirable qualities.

One day, when most of the others were on deck and it was just him and the kid in their bunks, he handed Tommy that letter and asked him to read it.

"Why don't you read it yourself?" Tommy asked. There wasn't any complaint in his tone, but only curiosity that Cole had passed off the letter to him. He seemed more than a little surprised that Cole had even spoken to him. Most of the others left Cole alone. He couldn't seem to shoot worth a damn, judging by his performance on the rifle range at boot camp, but the kid had noticed that Cole had empty gray eyes that promised violence. "You haven't even opened it?"

"I'm seasick," Cole explained. "I can't see straight."

Tommy eyed him doubtfully. "You don't look so sick to me."

"Just do me a favor and read it."

The kid adjusted his glasses and then began to read, mostly because he was a little scared of Cole. The first line of the letter didn't help put him at ease.

DEAR CAJE,

Them two you killed had it coming so don't worry yourself none about it. I never did tell the sheriff, but I reckon he figured it out, anyhow. I am sorry that you got sent away to the army. Everyone says the war won't last long, so you should be home soon. The mountains will be pretty in the spring. I do want to thank you for what you done. Not every man would have stepped up like that. When you do get back, I hope that you will come around and say hello so that I can thank you proper. Who knows, I might even steal your clothes again.

Your friend,

Norma Jean Elwood

TOMMY HANDED BACK the letter like it was burning his fingers. He stared wide-eyed at Cole, but seemed to know better than to ask questions.

"Thank you kindly for reading that," Cole said.

"No problem," Tommy stammered, then got the hell out of there rather than returning to his bunk. Cole had told him in boot camp that his choice was between the Army and jail, but he hadn't said it was because he had killed two people.

Cole tucked the letter back into his pocket.

He smiled, thinking about the reference to stealing his clothes—

Norma Jean had done just that when they were barely more than kids, swiping them one day when he had gone for a dip in Gashey's Creek. Norma Jean promised to be quite a handful. He mused on that for a while. Since returning from Europe, he had not spent a lot of time worrying about women. He had been busy learning his trade, building his modest cabin on the hill, or just hunting in the woods. Well, he would indeed look her up when he got home.

Whenever the hell that was going to be.

CHAPTER FIVE

COLE HAD TRIED to imagine what Korea would be like, and he wasn't that far off the mark. He had pictured something more tropical, this being Asia, but Korea was a dry, brown, wintry place. Mountains raised jagged peaks on the horizon. No jungles that he could see. The whole country was a war zone, and Cole had seen war before—the burned buildings, the frightened civilians turned into refugees in their own country, and most of all, the mud.

What he had not counted on was the smell.

"Ugh, it smells like shit," said somebody next to Cole. He was exactly right.

As a country boy, Cole was no stranger to the smell of manure used to fertilize farm fields in the spring. Each kind of manure had its own peculiar smell—pig, cow, horse, even chicken. A farmer could tell those smells apart like a connoisseur could sniff a wine cork and tell you the vintage.

But the smell here was nothing like back home. No, it was much, much worse, for the manure that Koreans used to fertilize their fields was human. Something about using human waste seemed unnatural and unclean to the Americans and other western troops. In Korea, decades or even centuries of its use, all year round and on all crops, meant that the smell of human excrement pervaded the air and ground. The muddy fields exuded it.

All in all, Korea smelled like one big outhouse.

The man next to Cole made a face. "You know what? The Chinese and the Communists can have it. I doubt this place is worth fighting for."

"You might be right," Cole said. "But it ain't up to us."

They unloaded off the trucks that had carried them from the port, glad for a chance to finally stretch their legs. They found themselves in a sprawling camp filled with battered canvas tents. Ominously, several of those tents were marked with large red crosses to shelter the wounded. Even more ominously, artillery thudded in the distance, loud enough to vibrate up through the mud and twang their nerves. The sound of small arms fire rattled at the edges of their hearing.

Battle-hardened veterans marched by, their uniforms muddy, reeking of Korea, in some cases stained with blood. Some glared at the new arrivals in their fresh uniforms. Others laughed and bombarded the green troops with catcalls.

"Them Commies are gonna love you boys!" somebody shouted. "Fresh meat! They like to eat the ones fresh off the boat!"

Cole wasn't so sure that the soldier was kidding. None of the American soldiers thought of the Korean enemy as fellow human beings, but as occupying a lower rank on the evolutionary ladder.

Another soldier shouted, "Somebody take a picture! That's the cleanest looking squad I've seen in months."

Indeed, just about every soldier had a camera of some sort thanks to the Kodak company and also the cheap, but high-quality Japanese cameras picked up by troops on leave in Tokyo. Already, the Japanese economy was rising from the ashes and ruins. As a result, Korea had become a war documented with snapshots.

Some of the other men hunched their shoulders against the verbal insults, but Cole didn't mind. He had seen the same disdain for green troops in the last war. He knew it wouldn't be long before they were the ones doing the catcalling.

Silently, they marched toward the assembly area and formed up. Cole found himself in the front row, which didn't thrill him. He'd have been happier in the back. Next to Cole, Tommy Wilson had turned pale as a sheet and fell out of formation long enough to throw up. He ran to rejoin the squad.

"Take it easy, kid," Cole said. "This ain't an execution. The worst that could happen is that they'll march us straight to the battlefield. But hell, that's why you signed up, ain't it?"

"It's not what I thought it would be," Tommy admitted.

"It never is, kid. It never is. Just you wait, because it don't get no better."

They fell silent as an officer appeared at the front of the ranks. His uniform looked worn and well-used, but at least it was clean. He was tall, a couple of inches over six feet, with a sharp-featured, almost hatchet-like face and dark eyes showing under the brim of his helmet. Those eyes surveyed his new troops. From his sour expression, it was evident that he didn't like what he saw.

"Welcome to the Republic of Korea," the officer said. "I'm Lieutenant Ballard. In the days ahead, you will be placed in line of battle or other duties. You heard those boys giving you the business as you marched in—well, they've had a much worse time, believe me."

The lieutenant paused to wave vaguely at the mountains behind him. "You all know that you are in Korea, but more specifically, you are at the edges of the Taebaek mountain range. Here's the situation. We are going to occupy all of Korea and push the enemy back to the Chinese border at the Yalu River. If they love Communism so much, they can damn high-tail it into China."

A sergeant trailed the lieutenant. He wasn't as tall as the officer, but he had a heavy build and the look about him of a combat veteran. His eyes went from man to man, sizing them up.

The lieutenant nodded in the sergeant's direction. "Men, this is Sergeant Weber. Better to listen to him. He has saved my ass more than once."

Now, the lieutenant came closer, seeming intent on talking to some of the men individually. He approached Tommy Wilson, on Cole's left. "Can you hit anything if you're not wearing those glasses, son?"

"No, sir. Not really."

"We've got a war to fight and the best they can do is send us four-eyed soldiers." The officer sounded disgusted. "Keep your head down and do what your sergeant tells you, and you might just get back home. And whatever you do, don't lose those goddamn glasses."

"Yes, sir!"

Next, the lieutenant moved down the line. Cole stiffened. He found the lieutenant stopping right in front of him. "What's your story, soldier? You're not wearing glasses, but can you hit what you shoot at?"

"I try, sir."

"You sure as hell better do more than try, soldier! You sound like a goddamn hillbilly. You make moonshine or whatever back in those hills?"

"I reckon some do, sir."

"You reckon? Dear God, you really are a hillbilly. What do you think about that?"

"Whatever you say, sir."

The lieutenant clapped Cole on the shoulder. "You've got the right idea, son. Whatever I say. I've got to *say*, that being a bad shot is a disappointing quality in a hillbilly. I would have thought you'd have grown up shooting squirrels or possums. A soldier has got to shoot. You're going to get a lesson in that soon enough."

Cole felt relieved when the lieutenant moved on. He spoke with a few more men in the front row, and then returned to where he could address the entire unit. "This may seem like a big war, with artillery and planes and a hundred thousand Chinese troops massed on the border that we hope to hell decide to keep out of the war, but that doesn't seem likely. For you men, it all comes down to one man with a rifle. Corporal Heywood, step up here."

A man approached from the handful of staff that had been looking on as the lieutenant greeted the green troops. He was stout and sturdy, about five feet eight, and he moved with the natural ease of an athlete. What Cole noticed about the man was his rifle. Instead of the standard issue M-1 like the rifle that Cole and the other fresh troops carried, this soldier held a bolt-action Springfield equipped with a telescopic sight. Cole was more than a little familiar with such a weapon because he had carried one from D-Day to the fall of Berlin—and beyond.

The lieutenant spoke again. Cole had the feeling that this was not happenstance but that the sniper had been paraded in front of new troops before. The whole thing had an orchestrated feel. "This man here is a sniper," the lieutenant said. "All of you have had rifle training on the range, but I doubt any of you can shoot the eye out of a Commie at two hundred yards—all while he's shooting back. Corporal Heywood here can do that. Isn't that right, Heywood?"

"Yes, sir."

"How many Commies have you shot, Heywood?"

"At least twenty, sir."

Several of the soldiers around Cole gave a low whistle of astonishment. Most of them hadn't shot anyone—not yet.

"I can tell you one thing, men. It is true that we have those big guns and planes and napalm, but it is Heywood here who strikes fear into their hearts. Never underestimate the value of your rifle. The truth is, we are going to win this battle—hell, we are going to win this war—one bullet at a time. Make each shot count. And yes, I'm looking at you, Hillbilly."

Several of the men around Cole gave a low laugh, but Cole stared straight ahead, stone-faced. Sure, this sniper had shot twenty Chinese. How many Germans had Cole killed? Twice that. Maybe three or four times that. Each time, Cole had worked the bolt, chambered a fresh round, put the crosshairs on some man's head or chest, squeezed the trigger, watched him go down. Some men did that once during the war and felt haunted by it. Cole had done it again and again and again.

Enough times to keep him wide awake some nights, thinking about the enormity of ending so many lives.

No, Cole didn't laugh with the others. A few of the other veterans were just as grim. Those who had killed in the last war weren't so eager to do it again.

"Dismissed!"

They slogged back down the hill toward their new quarters.

Tommy had been standing beside Cole. Oddly, the kid seemed energized by the lieutenant's pep talk.

"Maybe they'll put us in the line tomorrow morning," Tommy said.

"I wouldn't mind having a chance to shoot some of the enemy. Combat can't be so bad."

"You'll see," Cole said.

Another soldier nearby overheard and spoke up, sounding annoyed: "What do you know about it?"

Cole didn't reply, but the kid did. "Cole was at Omaha Beach on D-Day," Tommy said. "He knows what he's talking about."

The other soldier snorted in disgust. "If you were at D-Day, and now you're here, then you are one unlucky bastard," he said.

Finally, here was something that Cole could agree with today. He laughed mirthlessly. "You got that much right."

"And you say that you're no good with a rifle?"

"Nope. Can't shoot straight."

"If you can't shoot and you're that goddamn unlucky to get sent here, then you'd better stay the hell away from me," said the soldier, whose name was Pomeroy. Cole knew that the man was also a veteran —he was also a loudmouth. He reminded Cole a lot of Vaccaro, who had served with him in Europe. He had been full of wisecracks, but you could count on him. Cole hoped the same was true of Pomeroy. When push came to shove, it never hurt to have someone you could count on to watch your back.

Cole glared at Pomeroy, who looked away from Cole's strange, cut-glass eyes. That soldier wasn't the first person to find Cole's gaze unsettling. Cole's eyes were hard to read, but there was something of the wolf sizing up his prey in that measuring gaze.

Pomeroy didn't buy it for a minute that Cole couldn't shoot. He grunted, "Can't shoot straight, huh? I call bullshit on that."

As it turned out, nobody had to worry about being too close to Cole out in the field. Their new sergeant had overheard the exchange with Lieutenant Ballard and caught on to the fact that the lieutenant thought Cole was a dumb hillbilly who couldn't shoot straight.

When orders came around that the mess tent needed a few extra hands, the sergeant volunteered Cole. He'd come all this way to fight the Chinese and here he was, hauling buckets of chow in a field kitchen under the command of a grumpy cook with a vocabulary mostly made up of a word that started with "f" and rhymed with "luck."

If it had been Tommy sent to work in the kitchen rather than to be a warrior, the kid would have been disappointed. But mess duty was just fine with Cole. He wanted to serve out his tour and keep his head down and return home in one piece. In this war, he wanted to be as different from his old life as a sniper as possible.

Hell, working in the mess tent, Cole didn't even need his rifle. He left it in his tent every morning. It was against regulations, of course, because they were in a combat zone and every soldier was supposed to keep his rifle within reach. Cole didn't care. His weapon of choice was now a soup ladle and that was just fine with him.

CHAPTER SIX

A FEW DAYS LATER, Cole's unit moved out, heading north.

"Anybody know where we're going?" Pomeroy asked.

"Just shut up and march," Cole said. "That's all you need to know." It didn't take a general to figure out that to the north lay North Korea, and beyond that, Red China, but Cole didn't feel like explaining geography to Pomeroy.

"You sound like you're from down South somewhere," Pomeroy said. "Hillbilly country."

"Yep, I am definitely a hillbilly. And you sound like you ain't."

"Definitely not," Pomeroy said. "I'm from New Jersey."

"I've never been to New Jersey," Cole admitted.

"The Garden State, which is like calling hamburger chopped steak, I've got to say, but it's a lot better than this place." Pomeroy shook his head. "You know why being in the infantry and being a mushroom are a lot alike?" he asked.

Cole wasn't biting, but the kid couldn't resist. Tommy asked, "Why?"

Pomeroy grinned. "We're both kept in the dark and fed a lot of shit."

"It sure as hell *smells* like shit," Cole said, crinkling his nose. The fields they passed through smelled foul with the stink of human waste spread as fertilizer. Of all the strange customs he had seen so far in his brief time in Korea, this one was the hardest to get used to. As a soldier in Europe, the customs and landscape had not seemed nearly as strange. "What do you reckon this place must smell like once summer rolls around?"

"No need to worry about that, Hillbilly," Pomeroy said. "We'll all be home by then."

"We'll see about that, New Jersey," Cole said.

Nobody knew for sure where they were going, but the entire 8th Army under General Walker was on the move from Pusan. The thousands of troops were divided among the several roads heading north because their sheer numbers would clog any single road. They were all now tributaries of the same river.

Sometimes, they moved by truck, although that wasn't any picnic, bouncing along the rough dirt roads on a bare wooden plank that battered your tailbone. After a couple of hours in the back of a truck, it felt like your joints were coming apart. Your bones ached and even your kidneys hurt. An Army truck wasn't any Rolls Royce, that was for damn sure.

Right now, they were marching, which was just fine with Cole. He carried a lot on his back, but still kept his head up to scan the countryside. The North Koreans were supposed to be on the run, but who knew when they would decide that they had run far enough.

Each man was loaded down with gear that included a rifle and ammunition, canteen, haversack, folding shovel, rations, and a down-filled "mummy" or fitted sleeping bag that was an improvement over the blanket that Cole had carried in the last war.

As if reading his mind, Pomeroy said, "Gonna get cold soon. That wind has got a bite."

"If we get up into them mountains, we'll be damn near frozen," Cole agreed.

It worried him that the soldiers lacked winter gear such as heavy coats, wool hats, gloves, and thick socks. Maybe they would get that gear once they were closer to those forbidding mountains. Then again, maybe not.

Soldiers liked to chew on a good rumor. Pomeroy had asked where they were going, and that was a question on everyone's mind. Some said they were stopping at the 38th Parallel that delineated the boundary between the North and South. Somewhere beyond that boundary was the North Korean capital city of Pyongyang. Maybe they were on the march to capture it. Others said they were going all the way to the Yalu River. On the other side of that river lay China.

Nobody had told them much beyond the officer's explanation. They were all mushrooms, just like Pomeroy had said.

Cole had at least some grasp of the geography. They moved through a relatively flat coastal plain, but the countryside was starting to develop some rolling hills. To the north, in the crisp air, he could just begin to make out mountains. These were not like the rounded peaks back home, but were jagged and more forbidding. They reminded Cole of broken knife blades. Cole hoped to hell that their path wouldn't take them through those mountains, but he wasn't counting on it.

To Cole's eyes, those mountains resembled nothing more than bare rocks scoured by the winter wind. There wasn't much in the way of tree cover to provide shelter. The Korean high country appeared arid and barren.

At their backs lay the Korea Straight that lapped against the shore near Pusan. To the east was the Sea of Japan. On the far side of the Korean Peninsula was the Yellow Sea. Just the thought of being in this distant corner of the world made Cole ache for home, to be in the autumn woods with a long hunt ahead of him. He was wondering if he would ever be able to go home again. The judge had thought Cole could return, so that was something.

"I got to say, I'm disappointed those North Korean troops ran off before we could teach them a lesson," Pomeroy said. "We came an awful long way to not get in a fight."

"You think they're done, huh?" Cole asked.

"The way I heard it, those North Korean troops are scattered to the four winds. We scared them off."

"Let's hope so," Cole said. "But I've got to ask you something. You say you're from New Jersey?"

"The Garden State, remember."

"If you say so," Cole said. "But let me ask you this. If a bunch of enemy soldiers started marching into New Jersey, would you run off or would you fight?"

"What kind of a dumbass question is that?" Pomeroy said. "I'd fight, of course."

Cole nodded. "That's what I thought. Keeping that in mind, maybe we ain't seen the last of the North Koreans—or maybe of their Chinese friends, neither."

"Those slant-eyed bastards couldn't fight their way out of a rice paper bag."

Having fought Germans and Russians, Cole wasn't as quick to dismiss the North Koreans or the Chinese just because they hadn't encountered any yet. "We'll see."

The miles wore on. After the long trip from the United States, many of the soldiers were out of condition. Hell, a lot of them weren't in good condition to begin with. In the rush to get troops to Korea, boot camp had been too short to whip them into shape. These green troops hadn't done more than fire a rifle a few times. Boot camp was about more than weapons training, too; it toughened one up mentally and physically. A soldier who went through boot camp truly felt like a lean, mean, fighting machine. But that wasn't the case here. Many of the boys on this road had been eating their mama's cooking and sleeping in their soft beds scarcely a month ago. Now, they were expected to be hardened soldiers.

Cole looked around at the boys laboring under their packs, rifles dangling like forgotten appendages, and shook his head. If it came to a fight, they were going to discover their inadequacies in a hurry.

For veterans like Cole, who knew a thing or two about military life, more than a few of them had put on weight and gone soft in the middle. It was a rare man who had kept himself in condition. A peaceful existence didn't encourage it. Cole was an exception. His almost daily hikes up through the mountains had kept his legs muscular and his frame lean. He hadn't even smoked a cigarette in years.

"Where are those trucks?" Pomeroy griped.

"Shut up, Pomeroy. If you were in that truck, you'd be bitching about that. And keep your eyes open, will you? I got a feelin' about this place."

"Knowing you, it's not a good one."

One by one, the soldiers started to lag as the miles added up.

"Close it up," Sergeant Weber shouted, but it was a futile effort. Weber had a German accent that Cole found disconcerting the first time that he heard it. It turned out that Weber was an old Wehrmacht NCO who had washed up in the peacetime U.S. Army. He liked to say that soldiering was the only thing he knew.

Weber could bark all he wanted, and could even resort to swearing in German, but it did no good. The tired soldiers would pick up the pace for a short distance, and then fall behind again.

The column looked more like a shuffling mob than a company of soldiers, which was why the first shots from the field caused utter pandemonium. Ahead of Cole, a GI was hit and slumped to the road.

"What the—" the kid said, freezing at the sound of gunfire and looking around him in confusion.

Cole grabbed him by the pack and half-dragged, half-threw him into the ditch beside the road. Pomeroy was right behind them and jumped down beside them. A few inches of water sat in the bottom of the ditch, cold and stagnant, smelling strongly of the human manure used in the nearby fields.

"Christ," Pomeroy muttered, the knees of his pants now soaked. "What kind of war is this? I don't know which is worse, dodging bullets or liquid shit."

In leaping into the ditch, they were way ahead of the sergeant, who stood in the road, shouting, "Take cover! Take cover, goddammit!"

Without clear orders, some soldiers threw themselves flat on the road, while others simply ran in the opposite direction from the shooting. The fire from the field increased, and another GI went down.

While the majority of the men, including the noncommissioned officers and officers, had no real idea of what was happening, Cole assessed the situation through eyes that had seen his share of combat. It was clear that North Korean guerillas had set up an ambush, and very effectively at that. The Army troops had been taken by total surprise.

Lucky for the soldiers, there weren't that many of the enemy, and they were equipped with rifles. A machine gun or two would have been devastating to the exposed troops on the road. The road cut through open fields. There was nothing resembling cover except for the road-side ditches. In other words, the ambush had very effectively halted the advance and pinned it down.

"You see anything?" Pomeroy asked.

"They're on the other side of the field right across from us," Cole said. "Probably down in a ditch, burrowed in good. Can't be more than a dozen or so."

Pomeroy slid his rifle over the top of the ditch and opened fire in the general direction of the North Koreans.

Bullets snapped overhead. Another man was hit on the road and started screaming. Tommy was balled up in the bottom of the ditch, rifle clutched to him. He looked scared as hell.

"Easy, kid," Cole said. "Get up there next to Pomeroy, but keep your head down."

"I can't."

"Sure, you can," Cole said calmly. "You're a soldier. This is what we signed on for. All of us. Now get to it."

The kid crawled up next to Pomeroy, then put his rifle over the rim of the ditch. Cole went up behind him and put a hand on the kid's helmet, keeping it pressed low. "Just enough to see. Sneak a peek, like. Don't go sticking your whole head up."

"What am I shooting at?"

"Don't matter. Just shoot. Make them keep their heads down."

The kid began to return fire. He was shaking, so much so that his rifle jumped wildly each time he pulled the trigger. In his confusion, he started to rise too high above the edge of their cover. Again, Cole tugged him down.

"Hey!"

"What did I tell you, kid? Shoot back, give them North Koreans some lead to chew on, but keep your head down. You want a bullet to crack that pretty pumpkin head of yours wide open? We've got tanks and mortars to do the hard part."

Sure enough, they heard the deep boom of a tank lobbing a round toward the enemy. A geyser of dirt erupted, far beyond the ditch where the enemy was sheltering, but that gave the North Koreans something to think about.

The enemy fire slackened. More rifle fire was coming now from the Americans as the troops on the road, and those who had taken cover in the ditches, began to return fire. The return fire was wild and most of the men probably didn't know what they were shooting at, but it was enough to make the enemy keep their heads down.

Farther down the column, the tank fired again. This time, the round scored a direct hit on the North Korean position. The enemy fire stopped abruptly. Some of the enemy crawled from the ditch and began running away across the fields.

All at once, it was immediately clear that the enemy ambush had not been well planned because there was no fallback position or any cover for a retreat. The retreating North Koreans were now the sitting ducks—or running ducks—that the Americans had been exposed on the road.

Caught out in the open, several of the enemy fell under the American guns. Everybody seemed to be shooting, caught up now in the excitement of getting a shot at the actual enemy. They were blazing away like the worst kind of turkey shoot, with the exception of Cole. He contented himself with watching the action as the tank and then the small arms fire finally beat the hell out of the North Koreans and sent them scurrying. One by one, the enemy fell dead until there weren't any upright, running targets on the field.

Just as quickly as it had begun, the ambush was now over.

But all around them, the shooting hadn't stopped. Cole scanned the surrounding fields, but he didn't see anything. What the hell was everybody shooting at?

CHAPTER SEVEN

SOME OF THE soldiers were either so excited or frightened that they kept blazing away at the surrounding fields, although there weren't any targets. Their lack of discipline was a reminder that these were green troops. Worse, it was a reminder that some men had barely even gone through boot camp in the rush to get them into the field.

"Cease fire!" the sergeant yelled. The sergeant smacked a couple of the shooters on their helmets to get their attention. "Cease fire, dammit! *Verdammt!*"

Weber was able to swear in two languages, which was not only impressive, but also managed to make him sound twice as angry.

The shooting tapered off, but the silence did not last for long. From up and down the column came ominous cries of "Medic!" and the screams or curses of wounded men. The smell of gunpowder somewhat masked the stink from the fields. A couple of soldiers lay still in the road, their blood soaking into the compacted dirt. It didn't matter if they were green troops or veterans. They were dead all the same.

Down in the ditch, Tommy was still shaking. "I didn't do so good, did I?"

"You did fine."

"I froze up."

Cole shook his head. "You fought back, kid. You can hold your head up. It ain't easy coming under fire for the first time. The main thing is that you're alive, ain't you? Some of those poor bastards back there on the road weren't so lucky."

"Listen to him, kid," Pomeroy said.

"I guess you're right," Tommy said.

"There is one thing," Cole added. He looked both the kid and Pomeroy up and down. Cole had managed to keep out of the foul ditch water, but the other two were soaked through in various places. He grinned as he said, "You both smell like you crawled out of a latrine."

They climbed out of the ditch and made their way back to the road, where the sergeant was getting everyone organized. He was glaring at Cole.

"Goddammit, Cole. I had my eye on you. Let me see that rifle a minute."

Cole handed him the rifle. The sergeant reached out with a thick hand and touched the barrel, which was stone cold.

"You didn't fire a shot!"

"No, sarge. I reckon I didn't."

Sergeant Weber shook his head in disgust. "Some soldier you are."

"Pomeroy and Wilson covered me."

The lieutenant came over. "What's the problem, Sergeant?"

The sergeant glared at Cole. "Nothing I cannot handle, sir."

"All right. I need a detail to go with me to check those bodies. The captain wants to know if they have any intelligence materials on them."

"Intelligence materials?"

"Maps. Copies of written orders. Anything that can give us an idea about North Korean troop movements."

"Yes, sir." His tone expressed that he was doubtful that the dead attackers had any so-called "intelligence materials" on them. The sergeant fixed a baleful eye on Cole. "Take Cole with you, sir. He would be happy to go through the pockets of those dead gooks."

The lieutenant frowned. "I don't want to hear that term, Sergeant. You know what General MacArthur said about that word."

General MacArthur had officially banned any ethnic slurs that might create a rift with South Korean allies, but the word had even crept into official military dispatches. "Yes, sir."

"I'll need a couple more men."

Pomeroy stepped forward. "Me and Wilson will go, sir."

"Good enough. Let's get to it, then. Keep your eyes open."

The lieutenant started off, which gave Cole the opportunity to mutter to Pomeroy, "Don't you know better than to volunteer for anything in the Army?"

"If me and the kid didn't go with you, it's likely you'd get sent out here with a couple of guys who might shoot you by accident if they get jumpy. At least with us, you'll know that we shot you on purpose."

Cole grunted, acknowledging that Pomeroy was probably right about the likelihood of getting shot by one's own side. In the wake of the ambush, most of the soldiers looked anxious and trigger happy. In their eyes, every bush and shadow was now an enemy soldier.

They made their way back across the ditch and into the field. Once again, Cole was overwhelmed by the smell. Even in the cool weather, the place stank like the world's biggest outhouse. He kept scanning the horizon for threats, but if any of the North Korean guerillas had survived the assault, they were long gone.

When they reached the ditch with the dead attackers, Cole was somewhat taken aback by the appearance of the four bodies sprawled in the mud because the North Koreans were unlike any enemy that he could have imagined. First of all, three of the four were young to the point of being baby-faced. The fourth dead fighter was older, with a wrinkled, lined face. His dark eyes stared, unseeing. This must have been their equivalent of an NCO, he thought. None of the troops had on a proper uniform, but wore an assortment of dark clothing that to Cole's eyes resembled pajamas. Thin-soled shoes dangled from their dead feet. No helmets.

The lieutenant nodded at the bodies. "Get down there and go through their pockets and their gear. Bring me anything that looks like it might be written orders, or maps. We need to know what these people up to and where they might hit us next."

"Sir, none of them got away," Pomeroy said. "One thing for sure is that these guys here aren't going to bother us again."

"Go on and look, soldier," the lieutenant said.

Cole, Pomeroy, and the kid slid down into the ditch. Like the ditch on the opposite side of the field where they had sheltered, this ditch had at least six inches of foul water that was now mixed with blood and flecks of something meaty that Cole didn't want to think much about. Upon closer inspection, shrapnel from the tank rounds had torn some of the bodies badly. It was not a pretty sight.

The kid bent over and vomited. The smell of fresh vomit was now added to the stench. When he was done, he swiped at his mouth with the back of his hand and muttered, "Sorry."

Cole ignored him and began searching the bodies, concentrating his efforts on the older man, who looked like he would have been in charge. He didn't feel much compunction about going through the pockets of the dead man. His pockets were mostly empty, with the exception of a bit of string and a rag that might have served as a handkerchief. Not so much as a photograph or a few coins. Were these people really that poor? Hell, even the lowliest GI carried at least a photograph of a sweetheart or a deck of playing cards.

His search completed, Cole determined that the dead North Korean definitely didn't have any maps or written orders. He was no general, not even an officer. He was just a dead peasant with a battered rifle, dying for a cause that didn't seem to give a damn about him.

Up top, the lieutenant was smoking a cigarette, gazing toward the distant mountains. They had not made much progress on the road, but even so, those forbidding crags loomed closer.

"Hell of a country. I sure won't be sending any postcards home," the lieutenant said. "Find anything?"

"No, sir," Cole said.

"All right, come on up out of there. Let's take a look at the other bodies."

They clambered out of the far side of the ditch and made their way across the field on the other side, where another three dead men lay. These were the North Koreans who had fallen to the fusillade from the road, once the surprise of the initial ambush was over. They had been shot to pieces, hit again and again long after they had fallen by the trigger-happy soldiers. Again, their search of the dead came up empty.

Cole didn't exactly feel sorry for the dead enemy soldiers, but he could empathize with their plight. The ambush had been effective, but without any clear escape route for the attackers who had been caught in the open, it had also been basically a suicide mission, more an act of desperation than a military action. The poor bastards were just defending their home turf, even if they had the wrong idea about how that turf should be governed. No matter how you looked at it, Communism was a bad idea.

Here we are sticking our noses in, Cole thought ruefully. We ought to know better.

Or should we? Sticking his nose in had gotten him sent to Korea in the first place, he reflected. Then again, thinking about Norma Jean being helpless on the side of that road, he didn't regret his actions for a moment, although he could have done without the vacation to the Far East. South Korea was a fledgling democracy with the Communist bullies on their doorstep. They deserved someone to stick up for them.

They headed back toward the road, the lieutenant far ahead, not interested in chatting with the men. He was one of those aloof sons of bitches. The three GIs lagged behind.

"Those dead gooks were definitely something I didn't need to see," Pomeroy said. "Waste of time, anyhow. Kid, are you ready to go back home yet?"

"This isn't how I thought it would be."

"It never is, kid. Welcome to your baptism by fire."

"I didn't do so good during the fight," Tommy stated, bringing the subject up again. They could see that it was gnawing at the kid.

"It could be worse. You could be dead."

"I guess you're right."

"Hey, at least you shot at them. You probably killed some of those gooks back there."

"I guess," Tommy said.

"Cole here didn't even get a shot off," Pomeroy said. "I think that he's secretly a Communist."

The kid looked at Cole. "You *didn't* shoot, did you? Why is that? I know it's not because you were scared. You don't look like you're scared of much."

Even Pomeroy seemed interested in Cole's answer. "Yeah, I'm another one who'd like to know why you didn't shoot, Cole. Your rifle was stone cold. When push comes to shove and there's another fight with these gooks, we need to know that you've got our backs."

Cole thought about his answer. To his surprise, an answer didn't come readily to mind. Pomeroy had served in the previous war, but he and Cole hadn't served together, so the other man didn't know his history.

Cole wanted to tell them that he had killed enough for one lifetime, but he knew that wasn't the answer that they wanted to hear. It certainly wasn't the answer that they *needed* to hear. Besides, Pomeroy was right. If it came to another fight, they had the right to know that he had their backs.

"You can count on me," he said.

The words didn't sound convincing, even to Cole's ears. Maybe he really had lost his edge. The kid gave him a look and Pomeroy just shook his head in what appeared to be disgust. There was no further opportunity for reassurance because they had crossed the field.

"Hurry your asses up," the lieutenant shouted, climbing out of the ditch at the edge of the field and hurrying toward the road beyond, where the column was getting ready to move out.

CHAPTER EIGHT

MANY MILES from the American and U.N. troops crawling northward, Chinese troops were massed along the north bank of the Yalu River that defined the boundary between China and North Korea.

A company of these troops was assembled on a flat plain with the Yalu sparking in the autumn light and the dark, brooding Taebaek mountains beyond.

The assembled men wore the Chinese quilted field hats, similar to the Russian ushanka. Unlike U.N. troops, the Chinese did not wear helmets. The soft hats would not stop shrapnel, but they offered protection against the cold, which was just as deadly.

An officer stood before them, watching the men expectantly. The soldiers stood at attention, their gazes at a point fixed above his head. He stood with a bottle of booze in one hand and a pair of boots in the other, holding them at arm's length. It wasn't that the officer was drinking the booze or wearing the boots. Instead, these were being offered as prizes of some sort.

This was such an unusual sight that all of the Chinese soldiers stood transfixed. Beyond them was a shooting range that had been set up, evidently for this demonstration, or whatever it was that the officer had planned. In the field before the men, a single post had been set at one end of the range. Chen Zhijun might have expected an execution, except for the fact that the post was set at target practice distance—and there was a target affixed to it.

"Sharpshooters! Step forward!" the officer shouted.

Chen hesitated. If he had learned one important lesson in Mao Zedong's army it was that one should never be eager to volunteer for any duty or put oneself forward in any way. One or two of Chen's comrades nudged him or whispered encouragement, but Chen did not move. He was taller than the average soldier and dropped his shoulders, trying to shrink and disappear.

"Sharpshooters!" the officer called. "You know who you are! Step forward before your comrades!"

Chen studied the objects in the officer's hands. Chen did not care much about the booze, but he knew that he could share it with the other men and they would thank him for it. It was the boots that he wanted. He recognized them as Soviet boots, heavy and warm, from their Communist brothers to the north. Winter was coming and the thin-soled shoes—barely more than slippers—that most of the men wore would not be much of a shield against the cold when the snow and ice arrived, as surely they would.

A few of his comrades continued to murmur, encouraging him. They knew Chen was a good shot. Most likely, they knew he would share the booze with them if he won.

Two men had heeded the officer's call and stood apart from the others.

Finally, Chen stepped forward.

He kept his face impassive, feeling the icy wind off the mountains brush his cheek as a reminder that autumn was coming to an end, and the bitter winter was beginning.

He did his best to stare straight ahead while also allowing his eyes to flick to the right and left, sizing up the competition. There was Liu and Huang, both strong shooters. They stood at attention and seemed to radiate confidence, their faces showing that they were only too happy for the chance to prove themselves. Proud men, both of them. And good shots.

But Chen had an advantage over Liu and Huang. He had been

trained in sniper tactics and marksmanship by the Germans before the start of what was known as the World War. Back then, in the late 1930s, the Germans had seen China as an ally and had sent them military advisors and equipment. Unfortunately for the Chinese, alliances had shifted when the madman Fuhrer supported the Japanese in their imperialist war of conquest. The Germans had withdrawn their advisors, Japan had invaded China, and thus began several years of horror for the occupied Chinese.

When possible, the Chinese had fought back. Chen had been one of those soldiers, turning his skills with a rifle against the Japanese invaders. Of course, the Japanese also had well-trained snipers of their own. The result was that Chen had fought a war of a hundred small battles, usually just him with his German rifle, often against small units of Japanese or even against Japanese snipers.

The Japanese had been cruel masters of China, killing or starving hundreds of thousands. Most of Chen's family members had been among the victims. War had hardened his heart.

When that war ended, he had sided with the Communists—the true Chinese, against those who fought with the Nationalists under Chang Kai-shek. Finally, the enemy had been defeated and exiled to Taiwan, leaving Mao and the Communists in control of China.

Since his teenage years, Chen had been at war. First against the Japanese, and then against the Nationalists. It was truly all that he had known.

Chen sometimes thought that his mission in life was to punish the enemies of China.

It was testament to his skill that he had somehow survived not just the war against the Japanese, but also the civil war.

Compared to the Americans or especially the Japanese, the Chinese people were by nature friendly, peaceful, even jolly, but years of war had made them grim. Under Communist rule, they now lived in fear of their own leaders, who had proven themselves far more ruthless than any Imperialist government.

The least of Chen's worries now was a shooting contest for a bottle of booze and a pair of boots. But in China, he knew there was no such thing as a simple contest. Everything was imbued with shades of mean-

ing. Every action resulted in a political reaction. Chen feared the
consequences far more than he feared missing the target.

"Good," said the officer, looking pleased. A commissar beside the
colonel, wearing such a crisp uniform. The political officer stared
intently at each man's face, as if trying to discern something there.
"We have the honor of having Major Wu here today to assist us."

The colonel handed the prizes off to Wu and motioned for a rifle
to be brought forward. Such was the paranoia of the Chinese Communists that they did not let their troops have access to weapons except
for training or until it was time to actually fight. The Communists
feared that weapons could be turned against those in power. Already,
their young nation was one based on control of the masses and fear. A
rifle in one's hands made any man the equal of those around him. The
Communists did not want any man to be empowered, but for all power
to flow from Mao.

Chen smiled to himself, reflecting that there were two things that
flowed downhill, water and *Lā shĭ* ... shit. This knowledge made him
wary of political officers and of this little shooting contest.

Liu went first. The target was a blank white sheet of paper affixed
to a board to keep it from fluttering in the wind.

The rifle itself was a Russian-made Mosin–Nagant, celebrated for
its accuracy. This one had an actual telescope, which was rare in the
Chinese military. Typically, Chinese troops were equipped with a
hodgepodge of weapons, many of them Russian, because the Communists did not yet have the industrial capacity to manufacture rifles. It
was not unusual to find Russian Mosin-Nagants, Japanese Type 99
rifles, and even aging Hanyang 88 rifles issued to the ranks.

Chen watched Liu take his three shots. He fired too quickly, in
Chen's opinion. Perhaps he was nervous. A soldier was sent down to
collect Liu's target. He came running back and presented it to the
colonel. The colonel studied the target, holding it up toward the sky so
that light was visible through the holes left by Liu's shots. The officer
squinted, as if he had trouble seeing the paper that was right in front
of his face. Chen, who had the eyes of an eagle, had no trouble see that
Liu's grouping could be covered by a hand.

Impressive. But Chen thought that he himself could do better. What about Huang?

They were about to find out. The colonel's adjutant deftly reloaded the rifle and handed it to Huang.

The man stood for a long time, rifle against his shoulder, one eye squeezed shut, as he sighted at the fresh target. Chen wondered if the man was waiting for his nerves to subside, or for the breeze to die down. The cold wind off the mountains blew intermittently. All of the men seemed to hold their breath. Finally, the air went still and Huang fired. Then again. And again.

When he had finished, the adjutant took the rifle and sent the runner down to retrieve the target.

Again, the colonel held up the target. Chen could see that the holes could be covered by a closed fist. He was impressed, in spite of himself. The men around him murmured, looking at Chen doubtfully, thinking that their chances of that bottle of booze had all but disappeared.

The adjutant nodded at Chen and put the rifle into his hands. The barrel, having already been fired, felt pleasantly warm in Chen's cold hands. To his surprise, the rifle looked relatively new, having all of its bluing intact. Considering that Chen had handled mostly battered weapons, he felt a trill of pleasure at firing a new rifle.

The runner went down and put up a fresh target.

Chen fit his cheek against the stock and pressed the rifle firmly into the socket of his shoulder. Being taller, the rifle fit him better than it had the previous two men, especially Liu.

Still, it was challenging to fire a rifle cold, without knowing its whims and characteristics. He understood the predicament that the other men had been in, and why Liu had fired so quickly and Huang so slowly. Chen kept both eyes open to improve his peripheral vision and depth perception. His fierce, dark eyes had been the last thing to see more than one enemy soldier alive. He settled his breathing, put the sight on the target, and squeezed the trigger.

The rifle fired. A chunk of wood flew from the post directly behind the target. A hit, then. That was something. He ran the bolt, and in rapid succession, fired two more shots.

He lowered the rifle and the runner went scurrying toward the post. He returned and handed the target to the officer.

The colonel squinted, holding up the paper. From this angle, Chen could not quite see the target, but he had glimpsed a hole that was not in the center. So, then. He had not won.

Beside the colonel, the political officer leaned in to whisper something in the man's ear. The colonel nodded, smiled, and pointed at Chen.

Hands suddenly clapped Chen on the back, but he was puzzled. Had he really won? How was this possible?

Chen found himself presented with the bottle of liquor, which he promptly gave to the men in his squad. They cheered happily. He kept the boots for himself, of course. The boots were sized to fit a Russian, which made them perfect for Chen's feet when bundled in winter socks.

No one made any move to collect the Mosin-Nagant from him. Chen looked around, wondering who to give the rifle to.

As the crowd around Chen melted away, he found that the political officer remained. Major Wu. Chen tried to give back the Mosin-Nagant, but Wu shook his head.

"Keep the rifle," he said. "You will need it soon."

"Sir?" Chen asked, puzzled.

But the officer only turned away to study the Yalu River sparkling in the distance, and then the mountains beyond. Chen realized that he had been given his answer. The time had come again to punish China's enemies. Those enemies would surely include snipers, and it had been determined that Chen was just the man for the job of confronting them.

CHAPTER NINE

IT WAS THANKSGIVING DAY, but Old Man Winter had already visited Korea. Snowflakes swirled in the hoary wind. Water froze in canteens. Wet feet turned black with frostbite in the night.

Cole never had given cold weather too much thought—it was simply something to be dealt with when one was out in the woods. You wore a hat and stayed dry. But this cold was insistent. It wormed its way into every gap and seam.

His unit, as well as others in the Eighth Army under General Walker, was finding its way forward slowly, heads bent against the wind. Their ultimate goal was the Yalu River, but enemy units had been reported between here and the river. No one had seen them yet, but the rumors had taken on shape and substance. Only General Almond and MacArthur himself did not seem perturbed—their orders to units in the field were to push on, no matter what.

So they marched on into the growing cold. Bone weary, Cole and the rest of the men were glad enough when word came for a halt. Surrounded by mountains, they were within a short march of the Yalu River. If they pushed hard enough, they could be on the Chinese border in a day or two.

"Don't get comfortable," the sergeant said. "The lieutenant wants foxholes dug. We have mess tents to set up, too—maybe we can get some decent hot chow for a change."

Considering that their rations were now frozen, that was welcome news. Pomeroy turned to Cole. "Mess tents? Sounds like we're gonna be here for a while."

"If we stay too long, we might freeze," Cole said laconically.

"You boys know what? It's Thanksgiving Day," Pomeroy said.

"Mmm, what I wouldn't give for some pumpkin pie," the kid said.

They all fell silent for a moment, thinking wistfully of the folks gathered around groaning tables back home. Dinner here in the frozen, Korean mountains did not seem nearly as promising, mess tents or not.

Adding to the misery of soldiers on the march, the deep cold had settled over the mountains and the remote valleys. Soldiers longed for the relative warmth that had greeted them when they came ashore weeks before. Had the weather changed that quickly? As they moved into the mountains, cold weather had marched down from the north to meet them. What the troops didn't know was that this cold wind had originated on the bitter steppes of Mongolia.

Soldiers put on whatever they could to stay warm—hats, scarves, mittens, extra socks, long johns. So much extra clothing made the march far more difficult, weighing them down and slowing their motions. The soldiers plodded now, rather than marched.

While the extra layers were welcome, they could also be a curse. The last thing that a man wanted to do was heat up too much and start to sweat. If that happened, he would start to shiver almost uncontrollably as soon as he stopped moving and his damp clothing turned chilly.

Pomeroy explained it to the kid: "The trick is to find a balance— keep moving, but don't break a sweat."

"Easier said than done," Tommy said, puffing under his heavily laden pack, assorted gear, ammunition, and rifle.

They didn't need to worry for long about standing around. The activity of setting up the camp wasn't much different from what men and armies had done in hostile country since time immemorial. The disciplined Roman legions might have done the same, setting up their defenses against the barbarian hordes. Supplies were unloaded, sleeping areas and guard posts were established, men looked forward to getting food of some sort into their empty bellies, and nervous eyes played over the surrounding terrain where any number of the enemy might be lurking.

One thing for sure, this cold and this country had not been welcoming—never mind the fact that they hadn't seen so much as a single enemy soldier since the ambush on the road. That didn't keep the rumors from flying.

"I got it from a guy in B Company that there's a hundred thousand enemy troops up ahead, waiting for us," the kid said.

"Is that all?" Pomeroy said. He gave a short laugh. "I heard it was a million."

The talk of enemy troops hidden in the hills made everyone jumpy. Even the officers looked uneasy—Cole realized they didn't know anything more than the men. From what little they had seen of the North Koreans, nobody was much worried about those particular enemy troops. But here in the mountains it made sense to move cautiously.

The objective now was to probe the rugged landscape and find these pockets of the enemy—and wipe them out. It never occurred to any of the men or the officers that events might go in the other direction—that it might be pockets of their own troops that would be targeted for annihilation.

In the distance, they heard the sound of approaching aircraft.

"Looks like cargo planes," Cole noted.

Pomeroy squinted toward the sky. "How can you even see them? You must have eyes like a hawk."

Soon enough, the planes came into view even for those who did not possess a sniper's eyesight. The three workhorses of the sky—the airborne equivalent of trucks—flew in a loose formation without any fighter escort. After all, it wasn't as if they had to worry about enemy planes. The approaching aircraft spotted the Army unit, circled, and came in low. One by one, crates were dropped, trailed by ribbons that expanded into parachutes. Curious men ran to intercept the crates as soon as they reached the ground.

Having completed their drop, the planes waggled their wings in farewell and started back toward their base at Inchon.

"What the hell?" Pomeroy wondered.

Some of the soldiers used bayonets to pry open the crates. Even from where Cole stood, he could smell something delicious. Thanksgiving dinner had dropped from the skies. It was a wonder.

Sergeants and officers arrived, along with the mess staff, bringing order to what might have been a free-for-all among the hungry men. Rough tables were set up on the spot and the cooks started dishing it out. Instead of using fine china, this meal was served out on mess kits, the metal so cold that the mashed potatoes froze and stuck to it.

The crates contained the complete makings of a Thanksgiving feast: roasted turkey, mashed potatoes, stuffing, gravy, cranberry sauce, pumpkin pie. For the hungry men, it was nothing short of a miracle. Providing such a feast to forces across the peninsula had taken nothing short of a logistical masterpiece, a testament to vast resources of the United States military.

"Happy Thanksgiving!" someone shouted.

"If somebody doesn't want their pie, I'll take it!"

"Yeah, right!"

"Hurry up and eat," someone else shouted, but good-naturedly. "If these mashed potatoes get any colder, you'll break a tooth."

The soldier wasn't far wrong. With the temperature hovering near zero degrees and the incessant wind, the turkey soon froze so that it had to be gnawed a bit in one's mouth. The mashed potatoes and gravy coming off the planes had been lukewarm at best. The cooks kept stirring the gravy to keep a skim of ice from forming.

A few of the luckiest soldiers got drumsticks that they could work over like a meaty popsicle.

Nobody complained. The soldiers cheerfully ate as fast as they could, trying to keep ahead of the freezing food. This was a taste of home, and it was a hell of a lot better than frozen C rations.

The feast did not last nearly long enough. Too soon, it was time to complete the work of establishing this position against the enemy.

"Back to work, boys," Sergeant Weber ordered. "I can guarantee you that the Chinese aren't sitting around waiting for us to finish our pumpkin pie." A few yards away, the sergeant motioned at Cole, Pomeroy, and the kid, then shouted at them to get busy.

"C'mon," Cole said.

He got to his feet, surprised at how quickly he had stiffened up in this cold. At least his belly was full. For Cole, who had grown up going to bed hungry on more than a few nights, a full belly was nothing to take for granted. "Let's get to work."

Setting up the tents proved to be challenging. First, there was the frozen ground to contend with. Between the frost and the rocks, getting tent stakes into the rocky ground was like trying to drive them into solid concrete. When possible, they resorted to anchoring the corner ropes to heavy rocks or even the scrub trees that grew on the arid plateau. Then the men had to wrestle the canvas into place against the icy wind. The fact that they had to work wearing gloves or mittens did not make the work any easier.

Despite the orders to get to work, nobody so much as groaned. Mess tents meant the possibility of hot chow, even after this miraculous Thanksgiving meal. Everybody was sick and tired of the canned rations. Unless you wanted to hack away at the frozen contents of a can, it was necessary to stuff these rations inside one's uniform, where there was at least a chance that body heat would keep the contents from freezing.

There was not much time to dwell on that. Now came the work of setting up camp.

The men set up tents and unloaded gear from trucks. Latrines also needed to be dug. Foxholes needed to be dug.

Cole unfolded his shovel and started digging. Although the ground was frosty, the dry, desert-like soil was fairly easy to dig. It was the rocks in the soil that gave them trouble.

"I haven't been this cold since the Battle of the Bulge," Pomeroy said. He looked at Cole and asked, "Were you at the Ardennes Forest?"

"Yeah," Cole said. The way that he said the word freighted it was all sorts of dimensions, all of them icy and wind-blasted.

"Now that was *cold*," Pomeroy said. "Thought I was going to lose my toes. That was bad. All that goddamn snow—not to mention German panzers. But I hate to say it, we may be in for worse."

"Pomeroy, I wish I could say that you were wrong, but I've also got a bad feeling about this weather. This ain't a cold snap. We're in this mess for the long haul."

Sergeant Weber spotted them talking and stomped in their direction.

"Here comes trouble," Pomeroy muttered. "The sergeant is still mad at you for not so much as firing a shot back at that ambush. You'd better keep your head down and your mouth shut, Cole."

"Don't I always?"

"Yeah, right. I got to say, for a quiet guy you always manage to say just enough to get yourself in hot water."

Weber looked about as cold and tired as they felt, which didn't make him any less cranky.

"Cole," he said. "I have been looking for you—"

"Looks like you done found me, Sarge."

"Always the wise ass, aren't you, Cole?" The sergeant smiled a crooked smile that managed to be as cold as the frigid air. "Well, I've got a job for you. The lieutenant wants a squad to go out and probe for the enemy. You know, make sure there's not a division hiding just out of sight below the next ridge. I said, 'Sir, if they run into that division then there's a good chance that squad won't come back.' He said, 'Well, then pick a squad of men you won't miss much.' Fair enough. Guess that's why he's an officer. Anyhow, you came to mind as being perfect to go out there and look for the enemy—seeing as how you might not come back."

"Thanks for thinking of me, Sarge."

"Oh, I was thinking of you, believe me. So pick a couple of men and reconnoiter, at least to the other side of that ridge."

"Gonna be dark soon," Cole pointed out.

"Then you had best get a move on, Cole. If you don't come back, I will assume that the whole damn Chinese army is out there."

"I'll take Pomeroy and Wilson, sir."

The sergeant glanced at the other two, shrugged. "It's their funeral," he said, then turned away, shaking his head. "If you see the enemy, hold your fire. Try to capture one of them, instead. That's why I thought you'd be perfect for the job, Cole. Rumor has it that you're not much on firing your weapon."

Cole watched the sergeant walk off, then turned to Pomeroy and Tommy.

"How 'bout it, boys?" Cole asked.

"Gotta die sometime," Pomeroy said. "At least I'll die full of mashed potatoes and gravy."

"Now, that's a true American," the kid said.

Even Cole cracked a smile at that.

* * *

AFTER STOWING THEIR EXTRA GEAR, the three men moved into the hills, leaving the American line behind. Once they had covered a couple of hundred feet, Cole stopped and looked back. The American line of defense that had seemed so reassuring when they were part of it, a viable bastion against the enemy, now looked insubstantial from a distance. The foxholes looked too far apart. The soldiers, trucks, and tanks looked puny against the backdrop of the foreign mountains.

Not for the first time, Cole had to wonder what the hell they expected to do here in the vastness of this land. The Thanksgiving feast had put him in a surprisingly winsome mood. It seemed strange that they now had to return to the business of warfare.

He forced his mind to focus on the task at hand. He kept his eyes roving over the landscape. It had gotten so cold that he had to leave his gloves on. He slipped them off now, deciding that he'd rather risk frostbite than not being able to fire his rifle in a hurry.

"What are we looking for, exactly?" Pomeroy wondered.

"Small, angry fellers with rifles," Cole said.

"You know any Chinese?"

"Hell, no. You?"

"No. What happens if we actually capture one of these sons of bitches? It's not like trying to talk to the Germans. At least you had half a chance of understanding each other."

"I reckon it's unlikely any of them know a word of English."

Back in Europe, most GIs had known a smattering of German

words. He'd heard it said that English was a distant cousin of German, anyhow. This enemy and his language remained a mystery.

Cole moved forward cautiously. A dusting of snow covered the ground, but his hunter's eyes did not detect so much as a rabbit track. Did any game even live up here? The brown landscape appeared desolate.

There wasn't much brush, offering little opportunity for cover to any hidden enemy troops. Scarcely anything grew up here, unlike the relatively lush mountains back home. The Appalachians were mostly soft, rounded, ancient hills. Covered in dense green forests. The mountains here had sharp ridges like the spine of a starved hog. The issue was that the landscape itself was so vast, full of hollows and ravines where an entire regiment could be lurking. The lieutenant had wanted reassurance that there weren't enemy troops hiding over the next ridge. But what about the ridge beyond that, or the next?

"Keep your eyes open," Cole warned.

"You think?"

Cole felt very exposed crossing the open slope leading to the nearest ridge. He signaled for Pomeroy and the kid to wait, then slipped his rifle over his shoulder using the sling and began to climb the last thirty feet toward the peak of the ridge. He tried to move quietly, but the loose gravel and soil didn't cooperate. If anyone was lurking on the other side, they would hear him coming.

Finally, he reached the peak and eased his head over. A long slope slid down into a ravine that was actually thick with brush. Already, the weak winter sun was getting low, leaving the copse in shadow. Another slope rose sharply on the far side of the ravine, pocked with the dark openings of shallow caves. He kept his head down, studying the brush and the distant slope. He strained his eyes, hoping for some telltale glimpse of movement. He didn't see so much as the flicker of a bird down in that brush.

But something didn't feel right. Cole had learned to trust his instincts. He listened to that strange part of himself that he had come to call the Critter. It was a primitive part of his brain that he didn't understand, other than that it was like that sixth sense that animals possessed, or maybe his cave-dwelling ancestors. What the Critter told him was that there was something hidden down in that ravine. He fought a sudden urge to get the hell out of there as fast as possible, forcing himself to watch and wait for a while longer. Finally, he gave up and eased his way back down to where Pomeroy and the kid waited.

"Well?" Pomeroy asked.

"I didn't see anything, but there's somebody down there, hiding in a big ol' thicket growing in the bottom of that ravine."

"Wait a minute. You said you didn't see anything. Did you hear something?"

"No, but I can tell all the same. We need to get the hell out of here."

Pomeroy studied his face. "Hell, you actually look spooked. That's got to be a first."

"Let's go." Cole started moving. "I got a bad feeling about this place."

"You know, your gut feeling won't be good enough for the sergeant, and definitely not for the lieutenant. Just say you saw something."

"You want me to lie and say that I saw a hundred of the enemy down there? I can't." In Cole's hill country accent, it came out as *cain't*. Cole knew Pomeroy was right that nobody was going to go on his gut instinct. But making up a story about enemy troops wouldn't help.

They retraced their footsteps, practically at a trot. The shadows gathered around them and grew longer. The sun slipped behind one of the mountains, abruptly plunging the plateau into twilight as if a shade had been drawn. The cold, dark night was coming on fast.

Reaching the American perimeter, they entered between the foxholes gouged into the frozen ground. Some of the men had gotten into their sleeping bags for warmth, leaving just their shoulders exposed as they peered over the rim of their foxholes. A few soldiers were already asleep, but no one seemed concerned about keeping their eyes open. The biggest threat seemed to be freezing to death. Cole wanted to shout at them that they had better keep their eyes open.

Accompanied by the lieutenant, the sergeant wanted to see them right away.

"Well?" the officer asked. "I hope you're going to tell me that there's nothing out there but more rocks."

"The ravine on the other side of that ridge looked to be empty, sir. But I have to say, it sure didn't feel empty."

Cole felt Pomeroy's glance, giving him a warning to keep his mouth shut.

"Did you see anything or not, Private? Is there a battalion of the enemy over there, waiting to attack us once it gets dark?"

Cole hesitated. "No, sir. Not that I saw."

Lieutenant Ballard nodded, then turned away to deal with other duties. Sergeant Weber caught Cole's eye and smirked, but stopped short of saying anything within earshot of the lieutenant. Cole was pretty sure that would come later.

When they had moved off, Pomeroy chuckled. "When are you going to learn, Cole? The lieutenant basically asked you a yes or no question, which you answered with *maybe*."

"Keep your eyes open tonight," Cole said. "I'm telling you that there's something out there."

CHAPTER TEN

COLE STUDIED the mountains in the fading light. The sight of the rugged landscape did little to dispel his sense of uneasiness. The trip to reconnoiter the surrounding ravine had put him on edge, but he thought that any trouble would come sometime in the early morning hours. Once it was fully dark, he crept into his sleeping bag, hoping to get some sleep. Pomeroy was already in his bag, bundled up so that only his face was exposed, dead to the world.

Cole couldn't blame him for sacking out. The biggest enemy at the moment was the cold. He had overheard the lieutenant saying that headquarters was predicting temperatures of 25 degrees below zero. Combined with the incessant wind, that made it some of the coldest weather that Cole had ever experienced. Even in the sleeping bag, Cole's body shivered constantly.

"You've got first watch, kid," Cole said.

"We have sentries out," Tommy said. "Why do we need to keep watch?"

Normally, with sentries on watch, the guys back in the foxholes could then sleep. But Cole didn't trust the sentries, so had set watches for their own foxhole.

"Did you or did you not come with me this afternoon to check that ridge?" Cole asked, snapping at the kid in a harsher tone than he'd meant to. It was a sign that he was as tired as the rest of them.

"But you didn't see anything."

"Just 'cause I didn't see the enemy don't mean he ain't there."

"You keep saying that," the kid said. "The sergeant and the lieutenant don't seem too concerned."

"The last thing they want to do is look like a couple of nervous Nellies and upset everyone," Cole explained. "Did you notice that the lieutenant doubled the sentries?"

"No, I guess I didn't."

"He's no dummy. He can sense it, same as I can."

"Sense what? You said yourself that there's nothing out there."

"Wake me up in two hours," Cole said, then spooned up against Pomeroy for what little warmth the man's sleeping body offered. Some of the men had been learning to do that to stay warm in this godawful cold, while others thought it was too strange getting so up close and personal. That was a foolish notion. It was just warmth, was all. Cole didn't mind because he had grown up in the cabin on Gashey's Creek spooning up against his brothers for warmth on winter nights. That damn cabin never had any heat. He'd done it with his dogs, too—but at least his brothers didn't have fleas.

Before he closed his eyes, he gazed up at the stars, as was his habit. The night sky was pretty much the same, all over the world, which was something to think about. *We all see the same stars, whether we are Chinese or Korean or American.*

His pa had taught him the stars. Pa was a good teacher and the best woodsman in the mountains when he was sober. Pa had eked out a living with a trapline, cutting wood, and making moonshine back in the hills. The trouble was that Pa liked his own product a bit too much. When he was drinking, it was best to stay out of his way. Making 'shine had even gotten him killed when Cole was just a teenager.

Cole had gotten his revenge, hunting down his father's killer. Revenge was something that ran through his being like a vein of iron through granite. He was a Cole, wasn't he?

The frigid sky was so crystal clear that the stars seemed to shimmer. Someone had told him that the stars were so far away that the light from them might be thousands of years old. He picked out Orion with his belt of three stars. Cole had always liked the constellation because his pa had told him that Orion was the greatest hunter that ever was—he could track his quarry tirelessly for days and when he finally drew his bow, he never missed. Cole could relate to that. He hoped that Orion sent some of that luck and skill his way, because he might need it before the night was through.

Cole slept fitfully. His own shivering kept jolting him awake

Near midnight, the noise of the attack woke him up for good.

* * *

AT THE FIRST strange noises filling the night, Cole came awake instantly.

"What the hell is that?" Pomeroy demanded, shrugging off his own sleeping bag and fumbling for his rifle. "Sounds like a fox hunt."

Pomeroy wasn't far wrong about the sound, although Cole wondered just how many fox hunts Pomeroy had been on in New Jersey. They heard horns—tinny bleats like you would indeed hear on a fox hunt—along with whistles and shouts. If Cole wasn't mistaken, there were even a few drums mixed in there. They peered out into the darkness, but they couldn't see a thing. The sounds echoed through the hidden peaks so that it was hard to tell exactly where they were coming from. To Cole's ears, it seemed as if the sounds were coming from every direction. He hoped to hell that he was wrong about that.

"What's going on?" the kid wanted to know. His voice sounded shrill and terrified, which was likely just the effect that the enemy out there in the dark hoped to produce with all those noisemakers.

"I reckon there were enemy troops down in that ravine, after all," Cole said. "That's what's going on."

This wasn't like fighting the Germans, who just opened fire without a lot of scare tactics. They had a job to do and were straightforward about it. Not a lot of what you would call fanfare. Considering that they hadn't seen much in the way of North Koreans, these must be Chinese troops. These Chinese wanted you to know they were out there in large numbers and let you think about that. There seemed to be an awful lot of marching around. They could hear indistinct shouts, but didn't understand a word. The foreign strangeness of it made the noise even worse.

All around them, the American forces were thrown into disarray simply by those horns, whistles, and shouts. Cole had to admit, the sounds coming from the darkness were scary as hell, like hearing a windstorm approach at night through the trees. You just had time to brace yourself before the first gusts hit.

"I don't know if they are coming at us or going around us, but be ready!" Sergeant Weber warned. He went from foxhole to foxhole, checking on the men, trying to reassure them. "If we are attacked, make sure you know what the hell you're shooting at. Don't just shoot into the darkness. We can't afford to waste ammo."

When the sergeant moved on, Cole turned to the others in the foxhole. "How are you fixed for ammo, Pomeroy?"

"I've got about a hundred rounds for this carbine," he said. "I was pretty sick of lugging that ammo around, but I've got to say, I'm not sure it's gonna be enough."

"How about you, kid?"

"I'm set about the same. What did you mean, Pomeroy, saying that it's not enough?"

"You heard the sergeant," Cole said. "Just make every round count. Make sure you've got a fresh clip in there, too."

The kid grabbed his M-1, grunting in frustration. "I can't get the bolt to work!"

Now what? Maybe the kid was just nervous and had forgotten how to work his weapon. It happened. Cole put down his own rifle. "Give it here," he said.

He took the other rifle and realized that the kid was right. The bolt was stuck solid, making the rifle useless.

"See what I mean?"

"Must be the cold. Froze the gun oil solid. I'll be damned. Ain't never seen the like."

This was a problem that had to be fixed in a hurry, judging by the sounds in the dark. Cole set the rifle butt in the bottom of the hole, being careful to point the muzzle away from his head, and then gave the bolt a sharp kick with the heel of his boot. It didn't budge, so he did it again. Finally, he felt the bolt give. He handed the rifle back.

"Thanks."

"After you put a couple of shots down the barrel, she'll warm right up." Cole turned and called into the darkness. "Check your weapons! The cold might have froze up the actions."

The guys in the next foxhole had a BAR with a similar problem. He heard them cursing as they struggled to get the weapon working. Cole hoped to hell it didn't take them long.

There was just enough ambient starlight that he could see the men positioned on his left and right. Their holes were about fifty feet away. Looking around him, Cole felt once again that the platoon was spread too thin. There was too much space between the foxholes and too many gaps. After all, this encampment wasn't meant to be anything more than a temporary defensive position before the American forces pressed on toward the Yalu. Judging by the noise to their front, it was too late to do anything about improving their defenses.

Spread thin. Limited ammo. Guns frozen in the cold. Well, *shee-iit*, he thought. *Gonna be a rough night.*

A new sound reached them. Or rather, it was something they felt rather than heard.

"What the hell is that?" Pomeroy asked, his voice pitched high.

"I feel that too," the kid said.

Cole held his breath, wondering what it might be. The ground beneath him trembled ever so slightly. Sometimes you felt that with tanks, especially when the ground was frozen like it was now, but Cole didn't hear any tank engines. What could be causing that?

Men, he realized. The feet of running men pounding the earth. Lots and lots of men.

"Must be thousands of 'em," he muttered.

"North Koreans?" Pomeroy wondered.

"We've walked across most of this damn country and haven't seen that many people," Cole said. "Where would they have been this whole time? No, those aren't North Koreans. They've got to be Chinese."

"Hell's bells," Pomeroy said.

There had been rumors that Chinese troops had been spotted, but no one had really expected to go to war with them. It was a hell of a war, Cole thought, when you weren't even sure yet who you were fighting.

He peered into the blackness, hoping for a glimpse as the running sound became audible.

They heard the sharp thump of artillery from the darkness, and the flash of guns. *They've got artillery? Thank God they didn't decide to soften us up first.* Flares arced up into the sky, turning night into day.

What Cole saw next took his breath away.

He thought at first that he was seeing things because the ground itself appeared to be moving. But it wasn't the ground in motion. He was seeing thousands of enemy soldiers trotting toward them, wearing strange quilted uniforms like a medieval archer would wear. The white uniforms made them almost look like part of the snowy landscape that had come to life like strange mountain spirits. The men screamed as they charged, adding to the shrill horns and whistles, creating a deafening din.

Cole felt his bowels clench involuntarily.

"Pick your targets!" the sergeant shouted. "Open fire!"

Cole put his rifle sights on the front ranks of the advancing Chinese. It would be impossible not to hit someone. He had shucked off his gloves in order to better operate the rifle. He squeezed the trigger, felt the rifle jolt. To his relief, the action seemed to be functioning well enough in the cold. He caught the flicker of the ejecting shell out of the corner of his eye.

Settled the sights. Fired again. And again.

It wasn't going to be enough. The Chinese opened fire. Most of them were shooting from the hip or pausing long enough to throw a rifle to their shoulders. It wasn't accurate fire, and fortunately most of the Chinese rifles seemed to be bolt action rifles, unlike the semi-automatic American weapons. Nonetheless, bullets began to whine uncomfortably close. There were just so damn many of the enemy. It was like the massed volley fire from the olden days of Redcoats and Colonials. Not too accurate, but after a while there was so much lead in the air that somebody was going to get hit. As if on cue, Cole heard the scream of a wounded man off to his right.

Finally, the Browning Automatic Rifle on his left opened fire, emptying its 20-round magazine on slow-fire automatic. The frozen action issue on the Browning must have been harder to solve than with the kid's rifle. The Browning opened up and cut a swath through the ranks of the oncoming Chinese. Enemy soldiers behind the ones that had gone down stumbled and tripped over the bodies.

Cole fired until he heard the ping of his empty clip ejecting, then moved to load another clip. He had left his hands bare to make the job easier, but in the awful winter cold, his fingers felt fat as sausages. He fumbled the clip, had to hunt for it in the bottom of the foxhole, then found it and slammed it home.

In the first minute, Cole reckoned that the devastating fire from his platoon had killed a hundred Chinese. The trouble was that here came another hundred right behind them.

"We ought to run for it," Tommy said.

"Stay put, kid. Ain't no choice here but to stay and fight. Get that bayonet on your rifle."

Listening, Pomeroy gave Cole a look that was hard to read, somewhere between determination and resignation, then fixed his own bayonet. His whole time in Europe, Cole couldn't think of a situation where bayonets had been used other than in training. But this was a different kind of war. A different kind of enemy.

More flares launched, illuminating the battlefield in a harsh glow as if a lightning bolt was stuck overhead. The Chinese were so close now that Cole could see their faces, contorted by the mixed fear and rage of battle lust. Every last one of the bastards was screaming at the top of his lungs.

"Goddamn," Cole said, awed at the sight in spite of himself.

They were about to be overrun.

CHAPTER ELEVEN

TIME SEEMED to slow down as the first wave of Chinese troops reached the American lines. Everything seemed to happen in slow motion, and yet not more than a few seconds had passed.

"Shoot the bastards!" shouted Sergeant Weber, who had clambered up from a nearby foxhole. He was armed with an M-1, and he stood there fully exposed to enemy fire as he emptied the clip at the Chinese troops rushing toward him. With the rifle empty, he started swinging the butt at the enemy soldiers. He managed to knock three down before one of the Chinese tackled him and both men went sprawling.

"I thought they'd all be dwarves," Pomeroy said. "You know, little guys. But some of them are big bastards."

Cole had been thinking the same thing. He had expected the Chinese to be small and slightly built, like the Japanese. But many of the oncoming Chinese were six feet tall, at least. Taller and heavier than Cole or Pomeroy. Their quilted jackets made them look even more solid.

"Makes 'em better targets," Cole said, and took aim again.

He fired eight rounds, and dropped eight soldiers. More Chinese swarmed in to take their place. The advance wasn't more than thirty feet away. He slapped in another clip as fast as he could, thankful for the rapid-firing M-1 in his hands. Lucky for them, the Chinese were too busy advancing to do much shooting. The next thing Cole knew, the Chinese were fifteen feet away. Then six. He fired at the soldier rushing toward their foxhole, screaming, bayonet fixed. The man kept coming, so Cole shot him again.

The empty clip flew off with its telltale *ping*. The bolt locked open. He was out.

No time to reload. A Chinese soldier charged toward them. Cole ducked down and grabbed the man's rifle, angling the bayonet away, dragging him down into the foxhole. Pomeroy smashed the soldier in the head with the butt of his rifle.

Another soldier ran at them and Cole grabbed him, throwing the off-balance man into the hole. This time, the kid was there, screaming like a banshee as he jammed a bayonet into the enemy soldier. The shy, uncertain kid had been transformed into a warrior by sheer battle madness. Pomeroy was busy wrestling with a soldier who had tumbled into the hole. Cole hit that one over the head and the kid finished him with the bayonet, grunting with the effort like a farm boy working a pitchfork into a stubborn bale of hay.

Still, the Chinese kept coming.

The thought crossed Cole's mind that this was crazy. In all his time fighting the Germans, it had never come down to hand-to-hand combat on this scale. This fight was becoming far more visceral.

Next door, somebody got the BAR working again and mowed down a row of Chinese directly in front of them. Pomeroy chucked a grenade at the enemy for good measure. No sooner had one soldier fallen, then another took his place.

Then Cole, Pomeroy, and Tommy just had time to reload before the Chinese were on them again. Cole emptied another clip at them. Beside him, Pomeroy and the kid fired their weapons madly, but with less effect. Pomeroy was having to shoot each attacker two or three times before he went down because the rounds from the carbine were less powerful compared to the M-1 rifle that Cole carried. He reloaded and dropped another eight. The hot rifle barrel burned his bare hands, but that was the least of his worries at the moment. If he stopped shooting, they would be overrun.

Another enemy soldier got through and dashed at them. Again, Cole managed to drag him down and let Pomeroy and the kid finish the job. The foxhole was actually filling up with bodies.

On their right, a Chinese grenade went off in the foxhole there. American curses and screams followed the flash and bang.

"We've got to get out of this hole," Cole shouted. "If too many of them come at us at once, we'll be sitting ducks down in there, especially if they toss in a grenade."

"I'd rather die on my feet, anyhow," Pomeroy said.

Next to them, the BAR went to work again and gave them enough breathing room to get clear of the foxhole. It gave good shelter from incoming fire, but it could just as easily become their grave if the Chinese swarmed it.

When the Chinese came at them again, they were ready. Cole knelt and got off another clip. He got to his feet and swung the rifle like a club. He knocked down a couple of the enemy, but then a big Chinese bastard who wasn't even carrying a rifle managed to yank the M-1 out of Cole's hands.

Cole drew his Browning and shot him. Were the Chinese actually sending some men into battle without weapons, intending for them to arm themselves with whatever they picked up off the battlefield? That was hard to fathom. He shook his head. Crazy. How did you beat an enemy like that?

He emptied the pistol, then tossed it into the foxhole.

The three men formed a loose circle, their backs to one another. The safety of the foxhole was just a few feet away just in case the Chinese did bring in machine guns or artillery.

More flares filled the sky, bathing the killing fields in a strange, otherworldly glow. Cole was relieved to see that the Chinese flood appeared to be abating. The question was, had they really made a dent in the attackers or had that sea of attackers simply gone around them the way that a river flows around an island?

He looked around, trying to get a sense of whether or not they were surrounded. He spotted GIs to his left, grappling with the Chinese much like they were. Those were the guys with the BAR, but it had fallen silent.

To his right, he saw bodies in American uniforms sprawled among many more Chinese bodies. He sure as hell didn't see any living defenders. As he watched, a Chinese soldier reached down, grabbed an M-1 from the hands of a dead American, and ran on. Cole swore, helpless to stop him. He didn't like the idea of being on the receiving end of an M-1's firepower.

Finally, the Americans had brought up mortars and a steady fire rained down on the oncoming Chinese. With the enemy packed so close together, the massed mortar fire had a telling effect. The shells exploded in the Chinese ranks, each mortar round so close that the ground shook. Any closer and they'd be in danger of the shrapnel hitting the GIs. He was thankful that the Chinese didn't seem to have anything but their rifles—and those damn horns and whistles, which were a weapon in themselves.

Cole grabbed a grenade, hurled it at a knot of Chinese, forcing them to fall back. Somebody nearby tooted one of those infernal horns and the next thing that Cole knew, he was face to face with a screaming Communist soldier. The man jabbed a bayonet at Cole's face, but he dodged it, drew his big Bowie knife, and slashed at the Chinese soldier. The man fell, hands at his face, and Cole bent down and poked the knife into the man's windpipe to finish him like he would a wounded deer.

"Cole!"

He heard Tommy shout for help and turned to see him grappling with a Chinese soldier, their arms and rifles all tangled up. His pistol empty, his rifle gone, Cole had no choice but to stab the enemy soldier in the side of the neck. The soldier let go. Screaming, the kid followed up with the bayonet, his skinny body contorted with the effort of forcing the weapon through the thick quilted uniform and then through the ribs of the soldier. He had to kick the soldier to get the bayonet free.

Cole turned again, his knife at the ready, but there were only a few stragglers now. The bulk of the assault appeared to have flowed off to their right.

The kid had his bayonet ready, but suddenly there weren't any takers. He seemed to be all in one piece, at least.

He glanced over at Pomeroy, who was listing to one side like a boat that was taking on water.

"You hit?"

"Just a scratch. I'll be all right. What about you? There's blood all over your face."

Cole suddenly felt the wet warmth of it and touched his face. He didn't hurt anywhere. "Ain't mine," he said.

From the gloom in the hills, those godawful bugles began to sound a different note. The Chinese whistles blew with a new urgency. With an overwhelming sense of relief, he realized that the Chinese had signaled a retreat. The flares fizzled and sank low on the horizon. In the last of their glare, he looked out across the plateau and saw mound upon mound of heaped bodies. You could easily cross to the ravine beyond by stepping from body to body and never touching the ground. He was more than a little astounded by the sheer numbers of dead Chinese.

The attack had been a massacre. A slaughter on both sides.

The more he thought about that, Cole was astounded to still be alive.

Darkness returned as the flares faded.

"You know what, Hillbilly?" Pomeroy was just visible in the gloom.

"What is it, New Jersey?"

"I'm gonna need some help, after all." Then Pomeroy slumped over onto the frozen ground.

CHAPTER TWELVE

COLE SHOUTED, "MEDIC!"

In the confusion after the fight, it didn't seem likely that they were going to get any medical help. Their position remained shrouded in darkness, but they could hear other cries around them for a medic—if any of the medics had even survived.

Although the Chinese attack had subsided, they could still hear random firing from the darkness.

Nobody showed a light because that would only have drawn fire.

Cole crouched beside Pomeroy. "Where you hit?"

"I've got so many damn clothes on, I can't tell."

"Where does it hurt?"

"My side. Feels like a hot poker jabbing me."

Cole prodded at Pomeroy's coat, found a rip, but not much blood. Using fingers stiff with cold, he tore open a field dressing and got it pressed against Pomeroy's side.

"Looks like a piece of something glanced your ribs," Cole said. "You're lucky."

"Hurts like hell."

Cole couldn't argue with that. "I reckon it does."

The biggest problem was that Pomeroy shivered almost uncontrollably. Hell, Cole himself was shivering. So was the kid. The temperature was so low that it would need an elevator just to get back up to zero. Now that the fight was over, the nighttime cold settled over them. What they needed was a fire to create some warmth, but there was no hope of that.

"Get inside your sleeping bag," Cole told him. "Got to use what body warmth you got."

"The last thing I want to do is get caught inside this sleeping bag if the Chinese come back."

"They won't be back tonight," Cole predicted. "We chewed 'em up good."

Pomeroy nodded, and struggled into the sleeping bag, muddy boots and all. The effort seemed to make him shiver even more. "Anybody got water?" he asked.

Cole handed him a canteen, but when Pomeroy shook it, there wasn't any telltale sloshing. Frozen solid.

"I'll be damned," Cole said.

"Here, I got some," Tommy said. "I had it tucked inside my coat."

"You're way ahead of us, kid," Pomeroy said, taking the canteen gratefully.

Cole and the kid worked to clear the foxhole of the enemy dead, stacking the bodies in front of the foxhole to create a low wall. It was gruesome work, but if the enemy attacked again, they might be grateful for the barrier. Once that was done, there was nothing to do but settle down and wait. Cole stared out at the darkness immediately in front of them, which seemed impenetrable, though he could make out the outlines of the higher peaks against the star-filled sky. Somewhere out there, the enemy was lurking, licking its wounds and waiting.

Meanwhile, the cold was the more immediate enemy. The bitter chill crept into any exposed gap.

"Better get into our sleeping bags, kid," he said. "Let's huddle up for body heat with Pomeroy in the middle. If the Chinese don't finish us off, this cold sure as hell will."

They both struggled into their sleeping bags. Between them, Pomeroy slept fitfully. The medic never had shown up, but judging by the sounds of suffering coming to them from neighboring foxholes, there were cases a lot worse off than Pomeroy.

Cole propped his rifle against the frozen edge of the foxhole and balled up his fists within his wool gloves, trying to keep his hands warm enough to function. After a moment's consideration, he slipped the rifle into the sleeping bag to keep it from freezing up.

"It's gonna be a long night," he muttered.

* * *

MORNING BROKE BITTERLY COLD, a few bands of pink showing between the clouds and mountains at daybreak. Cole was surprised to see Sergeant Weber limping over. Blood-soaked bandages wrapped one arm and one leg. Gray stubble on the sergeant's face made him look old and haggard.

"Sarge, I figured you was a goner," Cole said. "Didn't nobody tell you to keep your head down?"

" 'Reports of my death are greatly exaggerated,' " he said. "One of your American writers said that. Mark Twain. *Huckleberry Finn*. Besides, it will take more than a couple of Chinamen to kill me. How are you boys holding up?"

Cole ignored the sergeant's literary references, which he didn't understand anyway, and took stock. The sleeping bags had done their job, holding in enough warmth to stave off frostbite. Nonetheless, Cole's eyeballs actually felt like they might have a coating of ice on them. He blinked a few times to get them back to normal. Cole decided that he never had dealt with such intense cold.

"Pomeroy took a chunk of shrapnel across the ribs, but he'll live," Cole said. "Ain't that right, New Jersey?"

At the mention of his name, Pomeroy finally stirred. "Yeah?" he asked groggily.

"We called for a medic, but never saw one."

"Medics are in short supply," the sergeant said. "We lost a couple in the fight last night. I think the damn Chinese are targeting them. There's an aid station set up."

"What, and get out of this nice, warm sleeping bag?" Pomeroy shook his head. "I think I'll stay right here."

"You boys did good," the sergeant said. "We all did. We held our ground."

"As far as I'm concerned, the Chinese and the North Koreans can go ahead and have this forsaken piece of real estate," Pomeroy said.

"I agree," the sergeant said, surprising Cole. "But it's not up to us, is it?"

Once again, Cole wondered what they were doing here. Fighting the Germans had been so different. The objective had been clear: defeat Hitler and capture Berlin. What was their objective here? Who was even their enemy? The Chinese? Cole didn't know anything about them, other than what he could learn from the bodies all around them.

The sergeant started to walk away, then hesitated, seeming to think something over. "Walk with me, Cole," the sergeant said. "I'm going to check on the rest of the boys, and I might need a runner to take a message to the lieutenant, depending on what I find. My leg isn't much for running."

"All right." Cole was surprised at how reluctant he was to leave the relative warmth of his sleeping bag. He had kidded New Jersey about it, but the man had the right idea.

As Cole shrugged off the warm sleeping bag, the cold air slapped him. Now he knew how a newborn baby felt, forced out into the cold world. He paused to work the action on his rifle, making sure that it still functioned. The bolt snapped shut was a loud click that carried in the morning air. "Kid, look after Pomeroy."

"I don't need anybody to look after me," Pomeroy grumped. "What I do need is for someone to fix me a nice breakfast. Scrambled eggs, toast, bacon, lots of hot coffee."

"Good luck with that," Cole said. "Best you can hope for is a drink of water, if it ain't frozen."

Out of the foxhole now, Cole looked around. Now that it was daylight, the sight of so many dead was shocking. Here and there, he spotted a few American uniforms among the fallen, although a detail was already out, trying to retrieve the bodies. By far, most of the dead were Chinese.

In the cold, the faces of the dead on both sides had frozen to capture their final expressions. Some of the dead men's features showed surprise. Those were the lucky ones who had died instantly. Other faces had frozen into twisted agony. What bothered Cole was that many of the faces of the dead Chinese looked so young. Sure, last night they had been endeavoring to kill Cole and his countrymen, but they were just young men following their orders as soldiers. They were the enemy, but there was now a kind of innocence about them in death. Cole certainly took no pleasure in seeing them by the light of day.

The shock at the number of dead must have shown, even on Cole's face. He could be a hard man, but he had never seen such carnage.

"Pretty awful, isn't it?" the sergeant asked. "No matter how many we killed, they kept on coming. I wouldn't have thought much of the Chinese before last night, but I've got to say, they are determined."

"Never seen anything like it," Cole agreed.

"Come on," the sergeant said.

They made their way to the next foxhole, the one from which the BAR had done its deadly work. Three lumps lay in the bottom, wrapped in their sleeping bags. Cole thought at first that they were dead. Sluggishly, the three men waved up at them. Haggard eyes peered out from under frosty helmets and hoods.

"You all right?" the sergeant asked.

"Need ammo," one of the soldiers stammered.

"I'll see what I can do," the sergeant said.

"Any chance of something hot to drink?"

"I've got to say, coffee is scarcer than bullets out there," the sergeant said. "But maybe the cooks can get a pot going."

"Amen to that."

They moved on. "If we're going to win this fight, we are definitely going to need hot coffee and bullets, in that order," the sergeant said.

Looking around at the frozen landscape, Cole said, "Don't look promising."

"I was not joking when I said that hot coffee was going to be harder to find than bullets. We've got to worry about the cold as much as we do the Chinese."

"The cold don't run at you with bayonets, though," Cole pointed out.

"Yes, there is that."

He looked sideways at the sergeant, surprised that the man had singled Cole out to accompany him on these rounds. "Sarge, I got to say, I never reckoned that you liked me much."

Sergeant Weber snorted, causing a cloud of frozen breath to hang in the air before it was whisked away by the icy wind. "Back at that ambush on the road, I thought you were some kind of chicken shit. *Nutzlos*. Never fired a shot at the enemy. But then I got to thinking about it and realized that you weren't a coward. You were just keeping your cool, I guess you'd say. I see how you look out for that kid and even for Pomeroy. Anyhow, I saw you in action last night, Cole. You are no coward. You are a soldier. You never missed a shot."

"Everybody did what they had to do, or we wouldn't be here today."

"There was some talk, you know, about you being a hot shot sniper back in France and Germany. Any truth to that?"

Cole took a while to answer. "Maybe some. I ain't no hot shot, though."

The sergeant gave him a look. "You sure about that? I seem to recall some stories about a sniper named Lucas Cole. One of the best. Some say he ought to have the Medal of Honor."

"Same name," Cole agreed. "But I ain't necessarily the same man, anymore."

"That might be said about any of us that was in the last war, Cole. Hell, that was five years ago. Half a decade. There were a lot of times back then that I didn't know if I was going to live another half a minute. Hell, I was fighting all of *you*. Americans. Yet here we are."

"Yep," Cole said, surveying the bleak scene around him. "Can't say this place was worth the wait."

"Listen, Cole, what I wanted to say was that I told the lieutenant that you should be my replacement if some Chinese son of a bitch gets lucky."

Cole was taken aback. "Me?"

"Well, why not you? I'm half shot to pieces, Cole." Weber often struggled to hide his accent, but he sounded very German when the word *well* slipped out with a "v" sound. "The men need someone to lead them if the other half of me gets shot up."

"I ain't but a private."

"Didn't you get the news? That's the Army for you. Lieutenant promoted you to corporal this morning. Congratulations. A battlefield promotion. Good luck finding an extra stripe around here, much less a needle and thread."

Cole shook his head. "You better stay healthy, Sarge."

"I will if I can help it, but there you are just in case."

A sound reached down from the skies. Cole heard the whine of approaching planes. These had become far more familiar. Approaching at incredible speed, the Corsairs swooped low over the American position and headed for the hills beyond. A ragged cheer went up from the Americans. They knew what the enemy was in for.

All that Cole could see were the brown hills, but the pilot must have spotted a target. As he and the sergeant watched, transfixed, one of the planes dropped a payload of napalm. The jellied gasoline burned a strip of mountainside, black smoke roiling up. Something about the orange flames was far more horrifying than any artillery burst. It was hard not to feel sorry for the poor bastards on the receiving end of that, enemy or not. Cole shuddered.

They moved on to the next foxhole. Two men lay in the bottom, apparently sleeping.

"Price? Harper? How you two holding up?"

But there was no answer to the sergeant's question. Cole started to get a bad feeling about this one. Both soldiers were barely more than high school kids. They should have had someone more experienced out here with them—or maybe they had, and those men were now among the dead. Not that far away, a detail was retrieving the bodies of the Americans that had mixed among the Chinese dead. They were stacking the frozen dead like cordwood.

Down in the foxhole, Cole noticed that neither of the young soldiers was inside a sleeping bag, but they were huddled together for warmth.

"Hey!" the sergeant said, louder now. "You two lovebugs better wake up!"

Looking closer, Cole could see frost coating their eyelashes, the flesh of their faces white and frigid. There was no sign of blood or injury. They had survived the battle last night, only to freeze to death.

"They're dead, Sarge," Cole said quietly.

"Don't you think I can see that?" the Sarge snapped. But his anger immediately dissipated. He muttered, "Goddamn. How many others are we going to find like that?"

It was a good question, but the answer was going to have to wait. They heard the sound of more approaching planes, high above, but moving fast in the cold air. They both turned in time to see parachutes floating down from the planes.

"C'mon!" Weber shouted. "It looks as if somebody remembered us, after all."

Several other soldiers joined them as they ran for the rear area where the drop was taking place. The planes were low enough that they could get a good glimpse of them. These Fairchild Flying Boxcars were twin-engine propeller-driven cargo planes with a unique divided tail design—almost making the planes resembled a giant tuning fork. The fuselage ended in a wide cargo door, wide open as crates spilled from the hold. Surely, the Chinese could see the incoming planes, but not a shot molested them. Without any Chinese Air Force to speak of, the cargo planes approach unmolested. The cargo was being dropped at low altitude so that there would be little chance of missing the encircled Americans and accidentally supplying the Chinese troops instead.

The problem was that the crates were coming in too hard without enough time for the parachutes to slow them down.

"Look out!" someone yelled. Men scrambled to dodge the incoming crates.

Some of the cargo hit nearby small trees, snapping off the frigid branches with a godawful racket. Other crates hit the frozen ground and popped open.

Overhead, the planes were gone as quickly as they had appeared.

"Just like Christmas!" shouted a soldier, pawing through the materials.

After all, the troops were now desperately low on supplies. But the soldiers were soon disappointed.

"What the hell is this?" Sergeant Weber demanded, inspecting a crate filled with .40 mm ammunition. What they needed was more .50 caliber ammo. "It's the wrong damn ammo. *Scheisse!* If worse comes to worse, maybe we can throw this at the enemy."

Nearby, another soldier held up cooking pots. The entire crate was apparently filled with pots, pans, and cooking utensils. That was a hoot, considering that the soldiers barely had any wood for fires. "What are we supposed to do with these? Make soup?"

Weber reached into the crate and extracted a well-wrapped bundle. Pulling away the wrapping, he revealed a bottle of bourbon. "At least it's not a total loss, boys," he said, and handed the bottle off to a nearby soldier. "Somebody back there had some sense and was looking out for us. Share that around. It is not schnapps, but it might help take the chill off."

The sergeant started back toward the front line, Cole walking beside him. Most of the supplies, sent at great expense and effort, appeared to be entirely useless. One exception seemed to be several jerry cans of gasoline and some medical supplies. For the most part, they had just witnessed a typical Army SNAFU. Situation Normal, All Fouled Up.

"Looks like we're on our own," the sergeant said. "Word is that we are basically surrounded and cut off. The question is, how long do we have to hold out?"

"We ain't gonna hold out for long if the Chinese keep attacking like they did last night and if this cold keeps up," Cole said. They were coming back to the foxholes occupied by their own squad. Nearby, the burial detail was still moving among the dead, gathering American bodies stiff as frozen slabs of beef. He looked away. Cole shook his head. "We'll be down to bayonets and rocks."

"God help us," Weber said.

At that moment, a rifle cracked somewhere off in the surrounding hills, and one of the soldiers in the burial detail suddenly threw back his arms and fell over. The others dropped what they were doing and ran for cover.

"Sniper!" Sergeant Weber shouted.

Then he and Cole jumped down into the foxhole with the frozen soldiers for company, keeping their heads down as the sniper fired again.

CHAPTER THIRTEEN

HIGH ABOVE THE AMERICAN POSITION, Chen lay hidden among a tumble of boulders. A dusting of snow covered the ridge so that Chen's quilted white uniform blended almost perfectly against the landscape. It would take very keen eyes to pick him out.

"We should move closer," said Zhao. "You will waste too many bullets shooting from here."

"There's not enough cover down there," Chen replied, not bothering to take his eye from the rifle.

Much to his chagrin, he was not alone. Beside him lay Zhao, who had been assigned as his spotter. Of course, Chen was well aware that Zhao's role was as much spy as spotter. He was not a very good spotter, Chen thought, which likely meant that he was a better spy. He was certainly a creature of Major Wu. *There was a tiny bird who sang of what he saw.* The Chinese were jealous of giving any one man too much independence—especially a man with a rifle.

Another American plane roared overhead, but disguised among the rocks, Chen and Zhao did not present any sort of target. Even Zhao was not so much of a fool to move a muscle as the plane passed over.

He hated these fast-moving planes that gave the Americans superiority by daylight, forcing the Chinese to hide like rats. The pilots knew that there must be thousands of Chinese troops hidden in these hills, and yet they must have been frustrated in their search. From time to time, the planes did unleash bombs or napalm, but Chen had to wonder—had a Chinese soldier truly been foolish enough to show himself, or had the Americans bombed a rabbit or deer?

He was half-tempted to try to shoot one down, but Chen knew very well that would be an exercise in futility—one that might also bring the wrath of an American pilot down upon him.

Sighting in his Russian-made rifle, he fired again.

Another enemy soldier collapsed to the frozen ground and lay still.

"You got him!" Zhao announced, studying the scene below through a battered pair of precious binoculars. "Quickly, shoot another!"

"You are the spotter," Chen said impatiently. "Find me another target."

That shut Zhao up. He was soon occupied with glassing the enemy position. Not that Chen really needed him. Even without binoculars, he could see all that he needed to, although his field of vision was limited. Briefly, he wondered if he could get away with shooting Zhao in the head and claiming that the enemy had done it. He decided to see how the day went before he risked it.

He was nearly two hundred meters from the American lines. Chen possessed a much sought-after telescopic sight—such technology was a rarity in China unless it had been captured. Fortunately for Chen, he also had extremely good vision. Between the treasured rifle scope and his eagle eyes, it was a winning combination.

Once he picked out a target, he began to track the man using the reticule. He had adjusted the scope to allow for maximum elevation, but even so, Chen was shooting mainly by instinct. He had claimed many Japanese and many more Nationalists both with open sights and then the rifle scope. The Americans and their allies below were just another target.

Since before dawn, he had been in position with Zhao. He would have preferred to work alone, but he had been assigned a spotter. Today, he had felt that it would be easier for one man to hide from the planes, but so far, Zhao had not given them away.

The German snipers had trained him well more than a dozen years ago, but in years of fighting the Japanese and then the Nationalists, he had adopted some of his own tactics. It was German doctrine never to fire twice from the same position. Of course, German snipers had often fought in cities and towns, or in the enclosed fields of Europe. While constant movement made sense on some level—more than one shot from a position made it easier to pinpoint the sniper's position— it was also impractical in many ways.

Staying on the move did, indeed, keep the enemy guessing. That aspect of doctrine was sensible. However, movement also exposed a sniper. He had to leave his hiding place and find another. A good sniper would have his hides planned out, but there was still the business of getting from one to the next.

In this vast terrain, it was next to impossible to determine the source of a rifle shot. The crack of a rifle reverberated and echoed across the hills in confusing patterns. The Americans, for all their reputation as riflemen, seemed to lack decent marksmen. Given that reality, why make an effort to move?

Instead, Chen preferred to use a single hide as his sniper's lair. The Japanese also had highly developed sniper tactics, and like Chen, they had preferred a single place from which to pick off the enemy.

The attack during the night had left so many dead. He could see the corpses spread everywhere, mowed down by the enemy's guns. Although the Americans were fewer in number, their weapons were far superior. Throwing the Chinese forces forward in hopes of overwhelming the Americans now seemed to be a foolish tactic, but he knew better than to voice his opinion—definitely not in front of Zhao, who would only carry his words to Major Wu. In Communist China, one's words could ricochet and kill you as easily as a bullet.

The Americans were weaker now, having lost many men and expended much ammunition. The bitter cold also had taken its toll. Another attack tonight might prove more successful—and Chen had no doubts that this was exactly what was planned by the Chinese generals.

Until then, he would do his best to even the odds.

Sighting through the scope, he picked out a soldier running

forward from the rear area of the American position that was out of Chen's view. A messenger? Hitting a moving target at this distance was challenging. He put the sight on the soldier, fired. When he looked, he saw that the soldier was still moving.

"You missed!" Zhao cried. "I told you that you should move closer."

Chen ignored him. He ran the bolt, ejected the spent shell and loaded another into the chamber. The soldier was still up and running. Chen led him more this time, and slowly squeezed the trigger. The soldier sprawled in the churned ground. Zhao grunted in grudging admiration.

Chen nodded to himself in satisfaction. Bullet by bullet, he planned to punish the Americans for coming to this place where they had no business being.

He picked out another target, and fired.

* * *

ALONG WITH THE OTHERS, Cole didn't have much choice but to keep his head down as the Chinese sniper picked away at them.

But they didn't have time for this nonsense. The problem was that with daylight and the end of the attack, there was so much to do. Wounded needed to be helped. Weapons needed to be cleaned and tended, plus ammunition stocks distributed. Hell, it would have been nice to start a fire to try to keep some of the cold at bay.

But at the moment, the sniper kept firing whenever someone showed themselves. Some men tried to ignore the sniper—the rationale was that the son of a bitch couldn't get them all—but one by one the enemy sniper reaped an awful toll.

Back in his own foxhole with Pomeroy and the kid, Cole studied the distant ridge and wondered, *where the hell are you?*

"Someone's got to do something about that son of a bitch," Pomeroy muttered through chattering teeth.

"Got any ideas?" Cole asked. "With the echo, I can't tell where he's at."

"Somewhere up on that ridge."

Pomeroy was right, but the problem was that the ridge stretched for maybe half a mile, creating a rugged, natural hiding place for a sniper. The enemy could move easily from place to place, Cole was sure. Meanwhile, the American troops were limited to their foxholes, in plain view of the higher ground that the sniper occupied.

"The best that we can hope for is a muzzle flash," Cole said. "But it's awfully bright for that to stand out."

"Maybe the planes can bomb that whole ridge," Tommy suggested.

"Not a bad idea, but I don't think they want to use their whole payload to get one guy—if they're even lucky enough to get him."

Cole reached for his rifle. The sturdy M-1 had good firepower, but it wasn't what he considered a sniper rifle. More like using an ax to whittle, when what you wanted was a pocketknife.

Then again, you had to work with what you were given.

That included his current foxhole companions.

"Pomeroy, kid, I need your help to try and nail this sniper."

"C'mon, Cole. Get serious. You can't shoot what you can't see."

"That's just what you're gonna help me fix."

He explained what he needed them to do. Their job was to lure the Chinese sniper into firing at them by raising their helmets above the rim of the foxhole. They would use their rifles for that, rather than risking life or limb. Pomeroy would raise his helmet first, followed by the kid.

"Basically, you want us for bait."

"I reckon I do."

"Will he fall for it?"

"It's the oldest trick in the book, but maybe he ain't read the book yet."

"And you think you can actually hit him from here?"

"Maybe. Maybe not. There's only one way to find out."

Pomeroy sighed. "Let me get this straight, Hillbilly. We are going to attract the attention of the sniper so that he shoots at us. Huh. Did I tell you that you are one crazy some of a bitch?"

"Like you said, I'm a hillbilly. What the hell else do you expect but crazy?"

Grumbling, Pomeroy readied his rifle and helmet. "Say when."

Using his Bowie knife, Cole had gouged out a depression at the edge of the foxhole that would offer at least some protection. The frozen dirt was hard as concrete and difficult to hack through. He used his sleeping bag for a bench rest.

Cole's hard eyes scanned the desolate scenery. If the Chinese sniper wore one of the dirty white uniforms like his dead countrymen nearby, he would be damn hard to spot against the snowy rocks. But he had to try. He hoped for a muzzle flash, a glint of metal, anything to indicate the sniper's position.

He calmed himself and steadied his breathing.

"Now," he said.

Slowly, Pomeroy raised his helmet, creating a target. Since the sniper had first begun, most of the GIs were now keeping their heads down. Those who had tried to ignore the sniper had paid a heavy price. Some now lay sprawled in various poses of death.

"Nothing," Pomeroy muttered. "He's got to be damn stupid to—"

A bullet kicked up frozen clods of earth at the rim of the foxhole, some of the debris bouncing off the helmet. Pomeroy swore and fell back into the foxhole.

Frantically, Cole watched for any indication of the sniper's hiding place. A split second later, the sound of the rifle shot reached them and began to echo among the hills. The lapse between the bullet strike and the sound indicated that the sniper was a long way out. Cole turned his attention to the ridgeline to the northwest. If the tables had been turned, that's just where he would be, in that line of boulders because of the concealment they offered. Nobody would ever see him from the air.

Cole didn't raise his head off the rifle. His cheek felt welded to the stock. The rifle butt fit into the socket of his shoulder—or where it was supposed to be. He had so many damn layers of clothes that it was hard to tell.

"Kid, your turn. Raise up that helmet, but make sure you keep your head down. This son of a bitch can shoot."

From behind him, Pomeroy muttered, "I'm OK. Thanks for asking."

Cole ignored him and waited tensely as the kid raised his own helmet above the rim of the foxhole. Would the sniper fall for the same trick twice?

The answer came when the kid's helmet went flying, nailed dead center by the enemy sniper.

There. Cole thought he caught a glimpse of something up in the hills. Could be a flash of light off a telescopic sight, or maybe off a pair of binoculars. The glimpse happened too fast to be sure what, if anything, he had actually seen. Cole's brain did a million calculations in an instant, working off sheer instinct.

He aimed at the flash that hung in his mind's eye, then fired.

* * *

UP ON THE RIDGE, the number of available targets had dwindled as the Americans below grew more cautious. This frustrated Chen, who had already shot the ones who were brave enough or foolish enough to show themselves.

Beside him, Zhao had gotten to his knees. The spotter was glassing the American position through the binoculars with growing exasperation.

"You shot so many of the Imperialists, but now they are not showing themselves," Zhao complained.

"Perhaps they are not so stupid as we think," Chen said. He did not think that was true, but he knew that it would goad the commissar's canary.

All morning, they had watched the American planes circle overhead, hunting for targets. Farther to the south, they had watched cargo planes drop supplies for the American forces. Chen had assumed that these were drops of food, ammunition, and medicine for the wounded. However, the supplies and the men scrambling after them were far beyond his range.

"There is something!" Zhao said excitedly. "I see a helmet in that foxhole directly in front of us. Shoot him! Shoot him!"

Chen could see the foxhole, but he was really just guessing about the target. The front sight of the rifle blotted it out. But from the excited noises that the commissar was making, Chen suspected that the helmet was still in view.

He fired.

Beside him, Zhao was now half-standing, straining for a glimpse of the target through the binoculars. Chen worried that the pilot of one of those planes would catch a glimpse of him and get them both killed.

"There is another helmet," Zhao said.

"Get down!" Chen snapped, ignoring the fact that it was smart to stay on the good side of the commissar's canary.

"Down there! Do you see him?"

This time, Chen did. The helmet bobbed up higher than the last one. Were these Americans complete fools? He fired.

Almost instantly, Zhao fell down, a bloody hole visible in his overcoat. The man clutched at his chest, but a death rattle already gurgled in his throat. Then the sound of the rifle shot finally rolled toward them.

Chen slumped down, keeping low, so that he was almost face to face with Zhao's staring eyes. Considering that he had considered shooting the man himself, this was not an unwelcome sight.

Chen reached for the binoculars and put them into his pocket. With any luck, he would be believed when he claimed that the precious optics had shattered when the dying commissar had dropped them. Chen could use them alone in the field and no one would be the wiser. He left the body where it lay. If someone doubted the circumstances of the commissar's death, they could go find the body later.

However, it seemed impossible that one of the American soldiers had been able to shoot that far and hit anything—perhaps it was a lucky shot. But there had been just the one shot. Very intentional. It dawned on him that the men showing their helmets in the foxholes had not been fools. The Americans had a sniper of their own, and he had set a trap that Chen fell right into.

In his arrogance, he realized that he had seen the Americans as stupid and foolish. After all, Chen had stood against some of the very best Japanese snipers and then against the Chinese Nationalists. What did the Americans possibly know about his trade? But there was a man down there who was every bit his equal. Chen had let his guard down.

It wouldn't happen again, he thought angrily.

Perhaps he had punished the Americans enough for one morning. In any case, the attack that was coming that night would likely wipe them out for once and for all.

CHAPTER FOURTEEN

HIGH ABOVE THE FROZEN LANDSCAPE, a helicopter approached the isolated Army outpost. The helicopter resembled nothing so much as an ungainly insect, creeping awkwardly across the gray sky, its rotors beating a rhythm that echoed across the mountain ridges and valleys.

The thumping sound had earned these helicopters their nickname, *choppers*. The noise traveled for miles in the frigid air.

"That'll be the brass, coming to tell us to hold our position at all costs," Pomeroy said, sounding disgusted. "Chances are, we're not getting any help, either."

Cole reckoned he was right about that.

Someone had nicknamed these relatively newfangled aircraft "choppers" for the rhythmic sound their rotors made beating the air, and the name had stuck.

Slow and ungainly as the choppers looked, most officers preferred not to fly in them. Instead, they opted for a rough ride in an open Jeep across many miles of rutted road. That wasn't really an option for Almond, who was coming from too far away. His motorcade wouldn't have made it as far as the Army position, anyway. It was one thing to fly over the Chinese forces, and an altogether different thing to try to drive through them.

This particular chopper carried General Almond to the regiment headquarters. Almond could see the landscape below, but what he couldn't see were the Chinese troops hidden all around. If only he had, the outcome of the meeting that was to come might have been different.

It would have been easy enough for the Chinese to unleash heavy machine-gun fire or even sniper fire as the helicopter approached, but a few Corsair planes in the vicinity discouraged any such attacks. None of the Chinese wanted to invite a payload of napalm on their positions, so they worked to stay hidden during the daylight hours.

"There they are, sir," the pilot announced, pointing toward a cluster of military equipment. The equipment was almost swallowed up by the surrounding landscape.

"I see them," Almond said. If he had any additional impressions, he did not share them with the pilot.

The chopper settled to the ground, the wash of its rotors scattering dust and snow. Then General Almond emerged, surrounded by aides that included an Army photographer to capture any historic poses or handshakes, and hustled toward the command post. It was quite a show, but that was to be expected from General MacArthur's man on the ground in Korea.

In all fairness to Almond, he was known as an excellent administrator and had served MacArthur well. Almond had learned from one of the best. For all his faults, not to mention his narcissistic personality, MacArthur possessed glimmers of greatness. He had also proven himself highly effective at winning over the Japanese. Overseen by anyone else, the post-war occupation of Japan might have been a bitter disaster. But MacArthur had handled the situation deftly, creating a productive peace and strong ally. The question remained as the war grew more serious in Korea, was MacArthur still the old warrior or had he grown soft and complacent?

Almond had been a keen student of the great man, and overseeing operations in Korea was MacArthur's way of grooming Almond for something more. Almond's orders were to take troops all the way to the Yalu, and he would settle for nothing less, which was why he had ordered a chopper to fly him out. He wanted to see for himself exactly why all forward advances had stopped. Essentially, General Almond was MacArthur's direct emissary, which gave his presence added weight.

Tall and ruggedly handsome, Almond looked imperious next to Colonel McLean and LTC Don Faith, the commander and second in command of the regiment. Both of these other men looked exhausted and disheveled, having survived two nights of intense Chinese attacks. Although they had not been directly involved in combat, they had done their best to direct the defense against overwhelming odds. Both men were extremely competent and well-respected by their men.

General Almond entered headquarters and nodded at McLean and Faith. If he was at all taken aback by their appearance, he didn't say a word. He seemed to have just one item on his agenda, which was the advance toward China.

"What's the situation here?" he asked without preamble. "You look like you're settled in, Colonel. Your men appear to be dug in and have established defensive positions. This is not a stopping point. Your orders are to push on toward the Yalu."

The colonel exchanged a look with his second-in-command, then responded to the general. "Sir, about that. My men have hit quite a bit of resistance. We've got thousands of Chinese troops between us and the river. Just last night, we were almost overrun. My men need reinforcements and supplies if we're to hang on, never mind push on."

"Chinese troops? Surely you are mistaken. There can't be more than a handful."

Again, McLean and Faith exchanged a look, before the colonel replied: "General, perhaps you should ask them yourself. We have a couple of captured Chinese soldiers here."

Almond nodded, and the officers went into the next room, where the Chinese were being held. Both of the Chinese soldiers were quite young, barely more than teenagers. They wore the quilted uniforms that had become so ubiquitous to the men in the forward companies. Up close, the uniforms looked more like some version of long underwear than any sort of military uniform. Both men wore large tags that identified them as "Prisoners of War POW" as if they were bundles of goods for sale at an auction.

Like their American counterparts, the Chinese POWs had suffered terribly in the cold. Their feet were now heavily bandaged due to frostbite. Olive drab blankets covered their shoulders. Neither man was restrained, and they both held warm mugs of coffee in their hands, smiling as if they were very lucky to be here in this room, warm and bandaged and drinking something hot—and alive. Clearly, they couldn't understand a word of English, but they kept nodding reassuringly at the faces standing over them.

Although their comrades had delivered death and fear upon the American troops, the very last thing that these smiling young men seemed to be was a threat.

The colonel explained to General Almond that these men had been captured the day before, in the early morning hours. Apparently, they had become separated from their units in the confusion of the midnight attacks and had wandered aimlessly until stumbling into the American lines. The fact that they didn't have rifles had probably saved their lives. The prisoners had shared the fact that they had been sent into combat without any weapons, with orders to pick up rifles dropped by the dead or wounded. The Chinese seemed to have more men than rifles to arm them.

No wonder these poor bastards had been happy to surrender.

"So that's the enemy?" Almond asked in disbelief. Like a lot of career officers in the Pacific, he had seen something of the Chinese military in the 1940s and had not been impressed. Like the men here before him, most of the Chinese soldiers had been poorly trained and underfed peasants. They had been defeated again and again by the Japanese military. He was incredulous that the commander claimed that more Chinese like these were blocking his advance.

"Yes, sir," the colonel said. "We have a couple of ROK officers here who speak a little Chinese, and they were able to communicate with these prisoners. They are from two different divisions. And they are positioned just out there."

The colonel indicated the surrounding hills with a sweep of his hand.

"Two divisions?"

"That is correct, sir."

Almond shook his head. If there really were two divisions out there, that meant as many as 20,000 enemy troops confronted around 3,000 U.S. and ROK soldiers under the colonel's command. Those numbers seemed too overwhelming to consider.

"Impossible," Almond said. "There are definitely not two Chinese divisions in front of you. Your orders stand, Colonel. You are to advance toward the Yalu River and the Chinese border."

"But sir—"

Almond put his hands on his hips and glared at the colonel. "Don't tell me that you're going to let a few Chinese laundrymen stop you."

The disparaging comment seemed to hang in the air. Colonel McLean, Lieutenant Colonel Faith, and the handful of other officers present stared in disbelief at the general. It was as if he hadn't listened to any of their reports about the huge numbers of wounded, the lack of food and ammunition, or dwindling numbers of combat effective troops.

Finally, the colonel said, "Yes, sir."

What General Almond had not shared with these Army officers was that he had delivered similar orders to the Marines on the western side of the Chosin Reservoir. The commander there, General Oliver P. Smith, had raised similar concerns about the overwhelming numbers of Chinese troops that his Marines seemed to be facing.

Like the Army regiment on the eastern side of the reservoir, the Marines had come close to being completely overrun, but had managed to hang on during the nighttime attack. Smith had asked for more men and supplies, but again, Almond was having none of that.

In a few days, when the Marines finally did pull out against the overwhelming odds, General Smith would famously state, "We're not retreating. We're just advancing in a different direction."

That time hadn't come yet, and all in all, the Marines were in a stronger position in that they had more troops and were better supplied. However, their position remained desperate enough. During the day, the Corsairs with their napalm and bombs kept the Chinese forces at bay, but at nightfall, the enemy would return in force to attack.

"Now that we've settled all that, let's go outside where the light is better," the general said. His tone changed, signaling that the strategy conference was over and that there were other things to discuss. "I want to recognize you and your staff for the outstanding job you have been doing."

"Sir?" the colonel asked, not really comprehending, but Almond was already outside. The colonel and his staff had no choice but to follow.

The photographer that Almond had brought along got into position as the general proceeded to present both McLean and Faith with Silver Stars. The medal was actually a large gold star with a smaller silver star in the center, suspended from a red, white, and blue ribbon. The award was the third-highest medal for valor on the battlefield.

Faith protested, "General, I don't deserve this medal. I've done nothing while the men in the field are the ones who held back the Chinese."

The colonel shot his second-in-command a warning look. This was sufficient to keep Faith standing at attention as General Almond pinned the medal on him. The photographer asked them to do it a second time so that he could get a better angle, but the entire ceremony was over in minutes because nobody wanted to linger in the cold. The temperature hovered at around fifteen degrees, but the incessant wind made it feel much colder. After the sun went down, the temperatures promised to plummet yet again to well below zero.

In the distance, they heard the sharp crack of isolated rifle fire. "What's that shooting about?" Almond wanted to know.

"Probably just one of those non-existent Chinese soldiers," Faith muttered.

Almond's face clouded. "What's that?"

The colonel jumped in. "The men are jumpy, sir. It's probably nothing. Then again, we have been taking periodic sniper fire. The Chinese have the high ground, so there's not much we can do if they want to pick us off."

"All right," Almond said. "Carry on, Colonel. I've got to get back. But let's be clear—there aren't going to be any reinforcements. I'll send you what I can in the way of supplies. Keep going toward the Yalu."

"Yes, sir."

At that, Almond and his small entourage made their way back toward the chopper, which was already powering up. McLean and Faith watched until the helicopter began climbing into the sky.

Then Faith ripped the new medal off his chest and threw it into the snow.

"Nuts to that!" he said.

"Sir?" A lieutenant was staring, perhaps thinking that his superior officer had lost his mind to have tossed away the Silver Star.

"I don't deserve this medal. It ought to go to one of those poor bastards in the foxholes." Faith paused. "Maybe one of the dead ones."

No one else even remarked on Faith's actions. Truth be told, they were all more than a little stunned by General Almond's parting words.

He hadn't come to save them or to offer reinforcements.

He was telling them to press the advance.

It was madness.

The general was leaving them high and dry, even as nightfall approached and the Chinese would surely send fresh waves of attackers.

CHAPTER FIFTEEN

S HIVERING IN THEIR FOXHOLES, the soldiers watched as the helicopter lifted off and shattered the frigid air with its rotating blades. Slowly, the ungainly craft picked up speed until it swept toward the south and disappeared. To a man, they suddenly felt quite alone as the stillness of the mountains returned. The quiet roared in their ears. Looking around at the surrounding ridges, and knowing that the enemy lurked there, made them feel yet more insignificant.

"Clouds moving in," Cole said. "Smells like snow."

"And just what does snow smell like, Hillbilly?"

Cole shrugged. He might have said *damp metal* or maybe *clean laundry*, if he hadn't thought that Pomeroy would just scoff at that. "If I got to explain it, then you ain't gonna get it, New Jersey," he said. "Just take my word for it that it's gonna snow."

Tommy spoke up. "One thing for sure, the planes aren't going to fly if it snows."

"You got that right, kid. If the Corsairs are grounded, I don't even want to think about what our Chinese friends will do."

The kid didn't have a response to that.

Earlier in the day, the sun had come out briefly and with it had appeared planes to harass the enemy. The bombs and napalm had kept the Chinese hidden and at bay. Once the skies were empty, the enemy would be emboldened. Since daylight, the Chinese army had left them alone.

One exception had been the sniper. Cole's shot had driven him away—with luck, maybe he had even nailed the bastard. But Cole remained unsettled that someone had been able to shoot with such accuracy at that distance. Cole's eyes were like an eagle's, and he was a good shot even with the M-1. That Chinese sniper had been just as good.

"Do you think they'll be back?"

Cole looked around at the hills where the shadows were lengthening as night came on. To him, it seemed as if those hills were holding their breath. Biding their time.

To the kid he said, "Ain't nothin' we can do about that but be ready. Wipe all the oil that you can out of your rifle so that it don't freeze up. Make sure you drink some water and eat something if you've got it. Don't just eat snow—that will just make you thirstier."

"Huh?"

"Your body uses more energy when you eat snow or frozen food," Cole explained. "It puts out more than it takes in, see? Keep a canteen and a couple tins of rations stuffed down inside your coat and there's at least a chance that it won't freeze."

The kid nodded. "If you say so."

"When was the last time you changed your socks?"

"This morning."

"Best change 'em again before the temperature drops."

Keeping their feet dry was a constant battle and more of an immediate threat than the Chinese. Officially, they had been told to change their socks every two hours. Needless to say, this was nearly impossible under the current conditions, but some attempt had to be made to keep one's feet dry if you wanted to keep your toes.

The problem was that soldiers had been issued rubber boots—galoshes, really. The heavy, ungainly galoshes weren't great for marching and were notorious for encouraging blisters. The boots weren't bad at keeping water out, but they also kept water in. In a warmer climate this may not have mattered, but in the subzero cold the boots became much worse than a hindrance.

The boots had a sort of felt pad in the bottom for insulation and to wick away moisture. In the extreme cold, however, that pad tended to freeze once it got wet so that their feet were essentially kept on ice. The best defense was to swap your socks as much as you could, keeping the damp pair stuffed into your coat so that it had some chance of drying out in your body warmth.

Cole glanced over at Pomeroy, who had drifted off but snapped back awake.

"How's that side?" Cole asked, nodding at where Pomeroy had been wounded in last night's fighting. The medics had patched him up back at the aid station and then sent him back to the line. There would be no sitting this one out. If the Chinese returned once the planes stopped flying at nightfall, they would be needing every man who could hold a rifle to fight.

"I'm too cold to feel a goddamn thing," Pomeroy said.

"I reckon that's good," Cole replied. "How are we set on ammo?"

"I've got five clips and two grenades," Pomeroy said.

"Kid?"

"Eight clips and four grenades."

"Jesus, kid, what are you saving up for? Christmas? You make sure you don't hold back if those Chinese come at us again."

"And they will," Pomeroy muttered.

"Yeah, it's likely. I've got even less ammo than you, Pomeroy. Damn. What did they say at Bunker Hill? Don't shoot till you see the whites of their eyes? That's the situation we've got here."

"I just wish I could've died someplace warmer," Pomeroy said.

"Stop with that talk. You ain't dead yet."

"No, I'm not," Pomeroy agreed. "And before I go, I sure plan to take some of these Chinese with me."

"Amen to that," Cole said.

They tried to get some sleep before nightfall, when they all knew there wouldn't be any chance of getting some shuteye. But they were cold and hungry, not to mention shivering so bad that it was impossible to nod off. Weber came around to see how they were doing. When they asked about ammo, he just shrugged. He didn't have anything to give them but encouragement.

Cole watched the shadows lengthen across the mountains, which made him miss home. The scenery here in Korea would have a haunting beauty if death and destruction had not lurked in those hills. One thing about the military was that it had given him the opportunity to see a lot more of the world than he ever would have experienced back home in Gashey's Creek. Then again, he might have had a longer life expectancy back home.

An hour before dusk, the snow that Cole had predicated finally began. With hardly any wind, dry snowflakes the size of silver dollars settled over the tense soldiers. In the fading light, the snow closed off the view of the mountains like a curtain swept across the stage. The snow kept on for several hours, burying the living and the dead alike. Cole was glad when it tapered off because the snow masked the movements of the enemy. From time to time, he heard a muffled shout or the ominous rumbling of a vehicle.

The kid heard it, too. "What's that?" he wondered.

"Keep your eyes peeled," Cole said.

It was midnight when they heard the bugles blaring in the hills above them. Crazy whistles echoed between the ridges.

All hell was breaking loose again.

"Here they come, boys. Whoo-ee. Get ready!"

"You don't need to tell me twice," Pomeroy grunted, getting into position. He had been sitting still for so long that Cole could literally hear the joints of the other man's body pop and creak in the cold. Pomeroy shouted into the darkness, "Come on, you sons of bitches! We're ready for you!"

Flares shot overhead, turning the night into day and illuminating the snowfall. Through the swirling snow, they could see the massed men coming for them.

The oncoming Chinese were making an awful racket. He heard horns, whistles, bugles, and angry shouts. The sounds were as frightening as the sight of the oncoming enemy.

What Cole couldn't see was the actual arrangement of the Chinese forces. These were organized into three waves. The first wave was comprised of men armed with the motley assortment of rifles available to the Chinese troops. By now, they would also be armed with whatever M-1 rifles and carbines they had captured from the Americans. The soldiers came on more like a mob than any organized military force.

Cole picked his target and started to fire.

What he could not see or know about was the second wave of Chinese troops. These men were largely unarmed, sent to follow behind the first wave and pick up the weapons dropped by the dead and dying. The Chinese had more men than guns.

Following the first two waves was a third line of Chinese, much smaller in number, but well-armed with pistols and even submachine guns. These were the political officers whose role it was to make sure that no one retreated from the attack. Advancing was the only option.

Cole felt a shudder go through him. There must be hundreds of the buggers out there, headed for the thin American line. With just a handful of magazines, how were they supposed to hold out?

"Better fix bayonets," Cole said, reaching for the weapon on his belt. He fit the bayonet to the muzzle of the rifle. He took out his Bowie knife and stuck it into the dirt, where it would be in easy reach. "Make every bullet count, boys."

A figure came running along the American lines, half hidden by the falling snow, going from foxhole to foxhole. Cole saw with surprise that it was Sergeant Weber. The son of a bitch must have a death wish, considering that the lead was already flying, like the first drops of rain in a big storm that was brewing. He handed them a handful of M-1 clips.

"Last-minute supplies, boys," he said. "Looks like the air drop did some good, after all, but it took a while for somebody to find these."

"Did you find more of that whiskey?" Pomeroy asked.

"Sorry, no booze this time. Just the bullets."

"We ain't gonna complain," Cole said.

The sergeant handed down several more clips of ammunition for their rifles, and then was gone to the next foxhole where the BAR was just getting warmed up.

The Chinese still hadn't brought up artillery, either because they didn't have any or the terrain was too mountainous to transport it, but tonight they had a lot more mortars. Explosions began to burst among the foxholes. Shrapnel whined overhead. Cole hoped to hell that the sergeant had made it to cover. Even if Weber wasn't his favorite person, the son of a bitch knew how to fight and they were going to need him tonight.

In the light from the flares, he could now see the seething mass of Chinese soldiers flowing toward them. Cole stared for a moment, mesmerized. Against the backdrop of fresh snow, the white uniforms made it seem as if the ground itself was flowing down the slopes toward the U.S. position. It looked like nothing so much as a human avalanche.

Some of the GIs started shooting, but the enemy was still too far away to do any good. Cole wished that he could tell them to hold their fire. Judging by the sheer number of Chinese, they were going to need every last bullet.

"Steady now," Cole said, as much to himself as for the benefit of the kid or Pomeroy.

"That's a lot of goddamn Chinese," Pomeroy said, his voice touched by awe. "Now I know how Custer must have felt at the Little Big Horn."

"You might not want to mention that, New Jersey," Cole said. "Things didn't work out so well for General Custer."

"At least the Chinese won't scalp us."

The human avalanche flowed closer. In the glow of the flares, Cole began to pick out individual faces. "Fire!" he shouted.

He put the sights on a soldier in front who appeared to be waving a sword—or maybe it was just a stick. He pulled the trigger and the soldier fell. His place was instantly taken by another enemy soldier and the flood advanced. Cole fired again, and again. More enemy soldiers died.

Beside him, he heard the crack of Pomeroy's rifle, then the kid's.

He hoped to hell that they were shooting straight. All around him blazed other rifles, flashing in the night. Off to his left, the BAR opened up again with devastating effect, cutting a swath through the nearest Chinese ranks. This was shaping up to be one hell of a fight, that was for damn sure.

CHAPTER SIXTEEN

HOURS before the second night's attack, Chen had waited with more than a hundred other Chinese soldiers, shivering in a narrow ravine under the cover of the scrub brush that grew at this altitude. Enemy fighter planes swooped overhead like giant birds of prey, waiting for any sign that would give away the hiding troops so that the Corsairs could rain bombs or burning gasoline jelly down upon them. Huddling together kept the soldiers warm and gave them all a certain measure of group courage to endure.

These men hoped to survive the day, only so that they could die that night, assaulting the enemy defenses. Chen would have been rueful at this thought if he did not hate the invaders so much. They must be driven away and punished, no matter what the cost. The Americans did not belong here. What did this business matter to them? The South Koreans who fought alongside the American imperialists were traitors. They should be helping their North Korean Communist brothers, not fighting them.

Silently, the men shared what meager food they had. Mostly plain white rice, long since cold, in a portion that scarcely filled the palm of their hands. It was not enough to sustain a man trying to stay warm in this bitter cold, but no one complained because that was a sure-fire way to coming to the attention of an officer or worse yet, one of the political commissars. Those fools always had enough to eat, judging by their snug uniforms.

Chen ate his rice silently, a few grains at a time. He had eaten less —and he had certainly eaten worse during the years of Japanese occupation. There was no meat, and certainly no vegetables, other than a few onions. Some of the men ate the onions raw, like apples. The Chinese did not have neatly packaged rations like the U.N. troops ate.

Chen kept his rifle balanced across his knees, staring up at the gray sky through the web of branches that provided natural camouflage. Ridges of hills surrounded them. It was a bleak and forbidding wintry landscape, but it was all the same to Chen, who had fought in many places. He could feel the man next to him shivering in the cold. They were all shivering. If only they could all get up and move around—but that would have meant certain death from above.

He felt relieved that no one had questioned the death of the commissar, shot at impossibly long range by an American sniper. In the end, the commissar's death was accepted as simply one of many and barely worth noting. He could still see the man's staring eyes that registered only a look of surprise. Chen realized that he had underestimated the Americans as soft and weak. One among them, at least, was a very good shot. As good as Chen, at least.

Chen was not one to think too deeply, but even he had to wonder, when had life become so meaningless? So easy to toss away? The Chinese had suffered for many years, it was true, under the Japanese and then through a bitter civil war. But now life seemed to have even less value, rather than more. What had this long struggle been about except to make it easier to die?

He pushed these bitter thoughts from his mind. Like the others around him, Chen closed his eyes and drifted off to a dreamless, fitful sleep. He woke after dark because a noncommissioned officer was urging them to their feet. A handful of men did not stir, and the noncommissioned officer kicked at them. They fell over into stiff heaps, never to rise again. The cold and lack of food had taken its toll.

In the safety of darkness, which had grounded the enemy planes, the Chinese troops emerged from their hiding places and gathered for that night's assault. Although Chen could not see more than a short distance into the darkness, he could sense the vast numbers of men around him, murmuring and moving in the night.

"Form up!" the officers shouted, working to get units assembled into some order.

Because Chen had a rifle, he was put into the first wave. If he was killed, then someone in the second wave would pick up his rifle. Chen had been in the first wave last night as well, and he tried not to dwell on the fact that he would be very lucky to survive a second night.

Not that he or any of the other soldiers had a choice. The third wave was really just a thin line made up of commissars, some carrying pistols and a few armed with submachine guns, making them some of the best-armed troops. Their job was to make sure that no one in the first two waves turned back from the attack. There was no way but forward.

"Chen, step out of line!" an officer ordered.

Looking to see who had singled him out, Chen recognized the young officer, Wu, who had been with them on the day of the shooting competition. He did as he was told. "Yes, sir!"

"You will not be in the first wave, Chen. You are a sniper. You will instead find a position west of the main column from where you can pick off the enemy during the attack."

"Yes, sir."

Chen was surprised, but he knew better than to question his orders. He had fully expected to die during tonight's attack. It was simply the way that things were. But now, he had been pointed in a new direction. He had been given a reprieve.

Chen moved to the edges of the formation, momentarily at a loss because it felt odd to have been spared from the direct assault. But the officer was right. His skills could be put to better use than as cannon fodder. Given enough ammunition and a good vantage point from which to shoot, there was no telling how many of the enemy he might claim. Chen welcomed that opportunity.

He crept closer to the enemy line, keeping to the higher ground. The other soldiers were forming on the far side of a ridge, keeping out of sight of the enemy. When the order came, they would surge over the crest of the ridge and charge down the slope toward the enemy, cascading like a waterfall.

Chen was blessed with keen eyesight that served him well, even in the darkness. Now that it was after midnight, the skies were beginning to clear and a few stars glittered in the deep black firmament. The snow that had fallen earlier that night reflected the starlight so that Chen could see for several yards before the landscape was swallowed up again by darkness. But with the clearing skies, the cold had descended once more. Chen's feet and hands and ears ached in the cold, but he did his best to ignore the pain.

Chen stayed well away from the main line of assault and picked a point that overlooked the American and ROK positions below. In fact, he wasn't all that far from where his shooting position had been earlier in the day.

The American position was largely dark, except where he could see the occasional glow of a cigarette. At least the Americans had cigarettes—that was too great a luxury for the average Chinese soldier.

He scoffed at the Americans' lack of discipline. As a sniper, those cigarettes alone would have given him plenty of targets. He fought the urge to target some of them now, and he settled in to wait for the main attack.

He did not have to wait long. Soon, the night was filled with the sounds of horns and whistles, then the shrill shouts of orders. Unseen in the darkness, Chen could sense the movement of huge numbers of men. The pounding of so many men on the frozen ground actually made the earth shake.

Then flares shot into the sky, finally illuminating the assault. Chen couldn't help feeling in awe of the spectacle spread before him. Looking out over the slope, he could see thousands of his comrades rushing down the hill toward the enemy. The ones in the front ranks carried rifles, and they screamed as they ran, knowing at any moment that the Americans would open up with their deadly automatic weapons. The Chinese could only hope to overwhelm them through sheer force of numbers, but the price paid would be heavy.

Behind that first line, the second wave of attackers followed, ready to pick up their fallen comrades' weapons and continue the assault.

The lucky ones in the second wave carried a few grenades, while some were empty-handed. Chen shook his head at the courage required to charge toward the enemy guns without so much as a weapon.

The third wave wasn't really a wave at all, but a thinly spaced line. These were the political commissars in their heavy wool coats and hats, looking more ready for the parade ground than the battlefield. But they were doing their job, all the same, preventing any of the soldiers in the first two waves from turning back. From time to time, Chen could see the burst of a submachine gun or the muzzle flash of a pistol as the commissars carried out their "motivational" work. He just hoped that none of the commissars wandered in his direction and started shooting at *him*.

On the slope behind him, he thought he heard footsteps. He swung the rifle in that direction, fearing that it might be American or ROK scouts. Then he heard a muttered curse as someone slipped on the snowy, sloping ground. Two men, he thought. Were they deserters?

"Do not shoot, Chen."

He thought that he recognized Wu's voice. "Sir?"

A moment later, Wu came into view, huffing from his climb up the slope. He had a young soldier in tow who seemed to be carrying a heavy box in both hands.

"I brought you ammunition," Wu said, settling himself on the ground beside Chen. Chen noticed that the officer spoke as if he had been the one who had carried the ammunition, rather than the panting young soldier. He waved a hand at the scene below. "Someone else can shoot the deserters tonight," he added with a tone of disgust.

Before tonight's attack, the soldiers had received a limited number of bullets. But that did not seem to be an issue any longer for Chen.

Wu barked at the young soldier to stay behind them and to keep an eye out for trouble. The young man did not have a weapon.

Then Wu took out a pair of binoculars and began to observe the defensive positions below. "You should target the machine gunners and mortar crews first. I will direct your fire. If you see any officers, you should shoot them as well."

Chen turned his attention from his own comrades and focused on the defensive positions below. He saw the enemy scrambling like rats as they prepared for the oncoming assault. A man stood, clearly visibly in the light from the flares. Chen guessed that he was an officer, perhaps giving orders.

He put his sights on the man and squeezed the trigger. The figure below crumpled.

He slid the bolt, then searched for another target. From above, he could see down into the foxholes so that the defenses did not offer much protection.

Off to his left, the first wave of the assault poured down the long slope toward the enemy. The roaring sound of the attacking Chinese gladdened his heart. He felt patriotic pride stirring in his chest. Then the enemy opened fire, tearing great holes in the advance. Tracers from the machine guns seared the night. His heart ached at the sight. But more than anything, he wanted to avenge those comrades who had fallen.

Chen turned his attention back to the targets below. He had a great deal of work yet to do.

"At ten o'clock from our position, there is a machine-gun nest," Wu said.

Chen's sights settled on the gleam of a helmet behind a machine gun. Again, his rifle fired, claiming another of the enemy soldiers. His sights returned to the American machine-gun nests below, and he squeezed the trigger.

CHAPTER SEVENTEEN

TONIGHT, the Chinese attackers seemed emboldened, as if determined to finish off the Americans for good. Maybe they'd had enough of hunkering down by day and hiding from the planes dumping napalm on them. Shouting and firing as they came, they seemed intent on finishing the job that they had started last night. A bullet snapped past Cole's head and he flinched, causing his next shot to go wide.

The Chinese were definitely within mortar range and he heard the thump of mortar rounds being fired from the American lines. However, the mortar fire seemed wildly inaccurate. There were also a lot of duds. What Cole couldn't know was that the severe cold had caused many of the mortar tubes to warp, affecting their accuracy. The middle of a battle was one hell of a time to discover the problem.

A few of the GIs launched rifle grenades at the attackers. Once they came close enough, they hurled grenades instead.

The problem was that the Chinese themselves were close enough to throw grenades. Their arsenal included stick-type grenades similar to what the Japanese and Germans had used in the last war. They also used a relatively crude type of grenade with a burning external fuse. The hissing grenades began to fall among the defenders, exploding with a deadly thump. From time to time, the Americans got lucky and the snow snuffed out the fuse. The snow did not affect the function of the American "pineapple" grenades—the problem was that they just didn't have enough of them.

"Jesus, I'm almost out of ammo!" Pomeroy shouted. "What the hell are we gonna do?"

"Pitch some grenades at the sons of bitches."

For the defenders, each foxhole had become like an island in a storm or a castle in a siege. Desperately, they tried to keep the swarms of attackers from overwhelming them.

This wasn't like fighting the Germans, who had approached each attack with an almost mathematical precision. The Germans had not exposed themselves needlessly, but worked forward using cover and suppressing fire. They had been tough and tenacious bastards who knew their business.

Cole was certain that if they had faced a German force this size that the defenders would have quickly been swept into oblivion—and most likely the Germans would have detailed a company to deal with the Americans while the bulk of the division went around them. But the Chinese didn't seem to have any strategy or plan other than to overwhelm the defenders through sheer force of numbers.

It was a strategy with a terrible cost, as shown by the bodies now piling up like snowdrifts in front of the American and ROK positions. So far, the defenders still possessed superior firepower thanks to the BARs and M-1s.

The Chinese crept closer, some of them literally leaning forward into the hurricane wind of rifle fire. More and more of them fell, but they kept coming, closer and closer.

Cole realized that the Chinese were within thirty feet of him. A soldier broke away and charged toward the foxhole, shouting and firing from the hip as he ran. Cole shot him, but the man kept coming, so Cole shot him again.

Beside him, Pomeroy grunted with the effort of hurling a grenade. "Down!" he shouted, just before the grenade went off uncomfortably close. But it had given the Chinese something to think about. For the first time, the attackers seemed to hang back.

But still, a few attackers broke away and ran at them. Cole fired at one man, but the second got within six or seven feet of the foxhole, so close that Cole's muzzle blast actually burned a hole in the soldier's white cotton tunic. Another grenade went off, pushing them back yet again.

Cole noticed a Chinese soldier sitting in the snow just a few feet away. Both of the man's hands gripped an ugly wound in his belly. The wounded soldier was looking right at him, saying something to him in Chinese. You could always pick out a word or two of German, but the Chinese sounded like raucous birdsong to his ears, like angry crows bickering. Did the man want to surrender? Was he begging for help? Cursing Cole? He shot the man through the heart, ending his suffering and silencing him forever.

Another soldier appeared, launching himself at Cole. From down in the foxhole, Cole jabbed at him with the bayonet, which caught in the man's belly and refused to come out. Screaming in agony, the soldier fell into the hole, his weight dragging Cole's rifle out of his hands. He grabbed his Bowie knife and slashed at the soldier's throat, finishing him, then wrapped his hands around the rifle stock and kicked at the body until the bayonet pulled free. Cole smelled blood and the tang of waste from the dying man's shattered bowels.

Someone leaped over the foxhole. Cole caught a glimpse of the puffy white uniform and fired at the man's back, sending him sprawling in the snow. When the man fell, he dropped something into the bottom of the foxhole. Cole realized that the soldier had been carrying a Bangalore torpedo, probably to use it against one of the trucks that was parked just inside the American line of defense. The torpedo consisted of a bamboo pole, from which dangled a silken bag filled with high explosives. A fuse sputtered and smoked, burning steadily toward the charge.

A Chinese grenade would have been bad enough. This was more like an actual bomb. They had maybe a few seconds before they were all blown to kingdom come.

"Look out!" Cole shouted, trying desperately to scramble out of the foxhole. Weighted down with gear and his rifle, he realized he wasn't moving fast enough.

"I've got it!"

Suddenly the kid was down in the bottom of the hole, scooping snow onto the fuse, which fizzled one last time and went out.

"You just saved our sorry asses, kid," Cole said gratefully. "Another few seconds and we would have been blown to kingdom come."

"I'm almost out of ammo," the kid replied.

"Me too."

Cole chanced a look over the rim of the foxhole at the enemy. Fortunately, Pomeroy had been keeping up a steady fire, but the Chinese were still coming.

"I've got an idea," Cole said, reaching for the Bangalore torpedo. "Have you got a lighter?"

"I don't smoke."

"Goddammit, neither do I. Trade places with Pomeroy. We need covering fire."

The kid leveled his rifle at the enemy and started shooting, while Pomeroy crouched beside him in the bottom of the hole. He saw at once what Cole had planned. "You are a crazy son of a bitch, Hillbilly," he said. "But it might just work."

"If we can send this bomb back at them, it could buy us some time."

Pomeroy fished in his pocket for his lighter. They had already shed their gloves and mittens in order to shoot, but now the backs of their hands were nearly frozen while their fingertips were burned from the heat of handling the hot rifle barrels. Pomeroy took out a Zippo lighter and struggled to get his stiff thumb to roll the wheel mechanism to strike a spark.

A Chinese mortar thumped nearby, showering them with snow and debris. "Dammit!" Pomeroy shouted. He dropped the lighter, then fumbled for it among the snow and loose rocks at the bottom of the hole. "That was close."

"Never mind that," Cole said. "Just get that fuse lit."

He picked up the Bangalore torpedo and tilted it so that his body sheltered it from the wind. On the third try, Pomeroy got the Zippo sparked. He held the flickering flame to the fuse, which was damp, and took a few seconds to catch. Finally, it started sputtering like a Fourth of July sparkler. Considering that the fuse had been put out once, he reckoned that he only had a few seconds.

He swung the end of the bamboo pole and hurled the Bangalore torpedo at the advancing Chinese.

"Down!" he shouted.

All three of them hugged the belly of the foxhole. At first, nothing happened, and the Chinese were so close that they could hear them shouting commands at one another. That reminded him to put both hands over his ears.

In the next instant, the air seemed to get sucked out of Cole's lungs and the ground jumped. *Boom.* A wave of heat and light washed over them. When they looked up again, the enemy advance in front of them was shattered. The enemy soldiers no longer came in waves—or maybe they had just moved on to find an easier position to attack the poor bastards there.

"That put a dent in them," Pomeroy said, his voice touched by awe.

"I reckon that wasn't the last of them," Cole said.

Unfortunately, he was right. All around them, the night was filled with tracer fire and muzzle flashes. Nearby, a BAR kept up its constant chatter and off the right, a machine gun let loose with burst after burst. Flares still filled the sky, so that there was no hiding the sheer numbers of Chinese.

Their respite from the battle was all too brief. A group of three Chinese soldiers ran at them, seemingly out of nowhere. Cole shot one, but the other two were suddenly upon them, leaping down into the foxhole.

Pomeroy clubbed one with his rifle. Once the man was down, he hit him again for good measure. The third enemy soldier was grappling with the kid, trying to stick a bayonet in him, but the kid had grabbed hold of the rifle and was struggling to wrestle it out of the Chinese soldier's grip.

Cole used the butt of the M-1 to smash the Chinese soldier in the head. The soldier let go of the rifle, then took a wild swing at Cole, hitting him with a glancing blow across the chin. The Chinese soldier didn't get a chance to swing at him again. Behind him, Tommy had picked up the enemy soldier's rifle and rammed the bayonet home. The man's eyes grew wide in surprise, and then he crumpled.

Screaming, the kid plunged the bayonet at him again and again.

"All right, kid, you got him," Cole said, taking Tommy by the shoulder. He reached for the rifle taken from the Chinese soldier and saw that it was an M-1. The sons of bitches must have scavenged it off the battlefield. "He had one of our rifles. Search his pockets. Maybe he's got some ammo."

The kid was still too stunned to react, but Cole pulled him down so that he wouldn't make a target. In the dead enemy soldier's pockets he found several clips of ammunition for the M-1. They were back in business.

He gave some of the clips to Pomeroy and kept the rest for himself. They started firing at any Chinese who charged their position. All too soon, Cole heard the *ping* as the empty clip ejected. He jammed in another clip and started shooting again. This wasn't marksmanship, he thought as he pulled the trigger again and again. It was slaughter. He didn't know enough about the enemy to hate them, or really know much of anything about them. He was shooting to survive. Kill or be killed. *Ping* went the clip again.

How much longer could they do this? Either until the bullets ran out or some Chinese soldier took a lucky shot.

In the distance, the bugles started sounding again. The Chinese attack began to ebb. Incredibly, although the Chinese troops were among them, all around them, as a matter of fact, they had not succeeded in completely overwhelming the U.S. and ROK troops, who were still holding fast. The Chinese soldiers began to retreat back up the slope. No more flares were fired, but as the light faded, he could make out small groups of retreating soldiers, many of them helping wounded comrades along.

"Good riddance," Pomeroy said. The voice next to him startled Cole. He had almost forgotten that he wasn't alone.

"You're still alive?"

"Just barely," Pomeroy admitted.

"Kid?"

"Yeah." The kid's voice sounded shaky, either from fear or cold—maybe a little of both.

"I just hope to hell that these bastards are done for the night," Pomeroy said. "If they attack again, we're all goners."

"Amen to that," Cole said.

A single rifle shot cracked in the distance from the Chinese side, and someone cried out from one of the nearby mortar squads. Some Chinese sniper was still at work up there.

"Keep your heads down," Cole said, mostly for the kid's benefit.

For the most part, the American guns had fallen silent, letting the enemy retreat unmolested. It would have been nice to think that this was some gesture, an *esprit de corps* between enemies, but Cole reckoned the truth was a lot simpler. The fact was that most of the Americans were just about out of ammo.

Pomeroy was right. If the Chinese returned, the Americans were all goners.

CHAPTER EIGHTEEN

AT DAYLIGHT, the scene that greeted the survivors of the attack was like waking from a nightmare that turned out to be all too real. Scattered around them in every direction lay the bodies of dead Chinese soldiers from the last two assaults. It might just be possible to cover at least half a mile, Cole thought, by stepping from body to body without ever touching the ground.

Judging by their contorted figures, many of the Chinese had not died peacefully. Their twisted limbs and bodies were now frozen into grotesque contortions. Cole gazed out at the carnage and shook his head. Sure, they were supposed to be the enemy. A few hours ago, these same men had been trying to shoot or bayonet him. However, seeing so much death did not exactly delight Cole, but just the opposite—he was struck by the waste of it all.

He wondered again what that Chinese soldier had been saying to him before Cole had pulled the trigger. Cole hoped that the soldier had been cussing him. He decided that was what he would believe, although he knew that he would also have a hard time getting that memory out of his head anytime soon.

He took a deep breath and pushed all those thoughts out of his mind. When you got soft was when you died. If he ever got home again, he could try to find some answer to all of this in the Bible or in long rambles through the mountains. However, the shores of the Chosin Reservoir in the Taebaek Mountains was not the place for self-doubt, not if he wanted to survive.

"Unbelievable," Pomeroy muttered beside him. "I wouldn't have thought it was possible, but this is worse than the first night."

"They were so convinced that they could overrun us that they kept throwing men at us," Cole said. "How are you holding up?"

"I didn't get shot again, if that's what you're asking."

Cole turned to Tommy. "Kid?"

The kid was shaking from the cold, so he only nodded and stammered, "I'm all right. I've never seen anything like it, though. It was like shooting zombies in a horror movie. They just kept coming."

"Ain't no movie," Cole said. "These ain't zombies. Just dead soldiers."

"An awful lot of dead soldiers," the kid said quietly, looking around.

"Everybody ought to change their socks," Cole said, trying to get the kid's mind on other things. "I know we didn't exactly get a chance to do it last night, what with the battle and all."

"Hillbilly, that may just be the understatement of the year."

The fact was that none of them had washed or changed their clothes, other than socks, in days. First, they had been on the march, practically racing to reach the Yalu River. And then all hell had broken loose. Simply staying alive was more important than hygiene.

It didn't help that their uniforms were caked with mud, soggy with slush, or stank of spilled diesel fuel. Pinned down by the Chinese and bundled against the cold, their innards made watery from eating snow or just from fear, more than a few soldiers hadn't made it in time when nature called so that they were forced to go around in soiled trousers. It had gotten so that nobody even commented on the smell. Fortunately, their own foxhole had been spared so far from that particular affliction.

Cole and Tommy started to undo the metal clasps of their galoshes, which wasn't an easy task because the metal was fouled with caked mud and ice. Cole thought that the kid's feet looked all right, and he nodded with satisfaction as the young soldier pulled on a dry pair of socks. His own feet had seen better days—not frostbitten, exactly, but definitely suffering from what the mountain people called chilblains—patches of waxy-looking skin that was painful to the touch. The fresh socks would help keep it from getting worse.

"Pomeroy, you ain't got your boots off yet."

"I can't," he said. Pomeroy hadn't even bothered to crawl out of his sleeping bag, which was pulled up to his chin as he lay in the bottom of the frozen hole. "If I take off either one of these boots, half of my foot will go with it. My damn feet are frozen."

"What the hell? You're supposed to take care of your feet!" Cole snapped, exasperated. "We can't carry you out of here."

"I can walk," Pomeroy barked back at him.

The kid spoke up, smiling for what might have been the first time in days. "Listen to you two, bickering like a couple of old maids."

Both Cole and Pomeroy glared at him and said in unison, "Shut the hell up, kid!"

The kid just shook his head and went back to staring at nothing in particular, way out in the hills.

"Sure you can walk?" Cole asked, more calmly now. "You ain't been out of this hole in a while."

"I can walk," Pomeroy insisted. "Besides, who said anything about us moving out? Looks to me as if we'll be here until the Chinese hit us again or hell freezes over—I'm not taking any bets on which one will happen first, by the way."

"We can't stay here," Cole said. He knew that they very well might; that they could be buried here for all eternity in this spot because they would never survive another Chinese onslaught. At that thought, the foxhole felt suddenly less like protection and more like a grave. "I'm gonna get out of this hole and take a look-see."

"Sure, go take a stroll," Pomeroy said. "Why don't you pick a few daisies, while you're at it?"

Cole scrabbled out of the foxhole, his limbs and joints stiff with cold. He slung his M-1 over one shoulder. He was down to his last two clips. If he got lucky, maybe he could scrounge some more ammo.

A handful of other men moved around, including Sergeant Weber. Cole was glad that the ornery son of a bitch had survived, even if Cole still didn't much like him. Cole would have been glad for a dozen more Webers if it helped to get them out of this mess. So far, the Chinese sniper who had annoyed them yesterday had not returned. Maybe Cole really had made a lucky shot and punched the yellow bastard's ticket.

He paused to sniff the air. It was a gesture not all that different from how a wolf might emerge from its den to smell for enemies. Cole felt better already out of the confines of that frozen hellhole where he'd spent the last two nights. It felt good to clear his head. No matter what Pomeroy said, he was worried about the son of a bitch. You couldn't march on frozen feet—not for long, anyway.

The sky had cleared, enabling the Corsairs to resume their patrols. They had been at it since dawn, dropping ordnance on anything that might remotely be a Chinese position. They seemed busier today, which might mean that the Chinese had become emboldened and less concerned about staying hidden—or maybe there were just a helluva lot more of them now in the surrounding hills.

He looked around at the snowy landscape of jagged peaks and valleys. The land looked almost newly formed here, jagged as shattered glass. Nothing grew except scrub brush and tough grass. Hardly worth fighting over, in Cole's opinion, and yet here they were.

He found Sergeant Weber standing over a foxhole, looking down into it and shaking his head.

"Frozen to death," Weber said. He'd heard Cole approach but couldn't seem to take his eyes off the scene below them. He muttered, *"Gott im Himmel."*

"Sarge?"

Cole didn't want to look, but Weber seemed to want someone else to see this. He could see three young recruits, curled up in the bottom of the hole. Frost covered their eyes and nostrils. They did not appear to be wounded, but none of them had sleeping bags or heavy coats to fend off the cold. Cole suspected that they had ended up leaving their gear behind during the battle, and somehow wound up in another hole. With so many Chinese around in the darkness, they had probably been reluctant to go back to their original foxhole, or maybe they couldn't even find it.

"They didn't have the right gear, that's for damn sure," Weber said.

"Nobody really does in this cold. Half these guys, their guns froze up on them."

"Got to wipe all the oil out that you can," Cole said.

"Yeah? Well, tell that to anyone you run into."

"Mostly we could use more ammo," Cole said. "If the Chinese hit us again, we'll be down to rocks and bayonets."

"What do you want me to do about it?" Weber snapped at him. "Why don't you write a letter to McArthur and see how much good it does."

"Whatever you say, Sarge."

It was no surprise that the sergeant's nerves were shot. He, too, had fought tooth and nail for survival these last two nights. Like his men, he hadn't had anything decent to eat. Also, he had the responsibility for the men in his unit—what was left of them, anyway.

Weber started to stalk off and then stopped. "Come on with me, Cole. I heard how you settled that Chinese sniper's hash yesterday. Keep your rifle handy in case another one of the bastards opens fire on us."

Together, they moved from hole to hole, checking on the men. Dead Chinese were scattered all around their positions. In daylight, it was disconcerting to see how close they had come to being completely overrun.

Many of the surviving American GIs were wounded, some quite badly. A few men had even lost arms or legs to Chinese grenades or mortars. Miraculously, they were still in the field. They had managed to survive because their wounds had literally frozen in the bitter temperatures, preventing them from bleeding to death. The medics had bandaged them up as best they could, then dosed them liberally with morphine to help with the pain. There again, the cold had left their extremities so numb that some of them couldn't even feel any pain.

"You ever seen anything like this?" Weber asked. "Maybe at the Ardennes Forest? Some of the guys said you were there."

"Yeah, I was there." Cole shook his head, thinking back to the winter fighting at the battle of the Bulge. "It was miserable, and it was cold and snowy, but not *this* cold."

"Some of these poor bastards tried to at least get warm at the aid station, but you know what? As soon as they warmed up, they started bleeding again. There was really no help for them and more than a few died. It's a hell of a thing."

Cole had to agree. His heart went out to the wounded men. They were on borrowed time. The aid station wasn't more than a couple of drafty tents with a little bit of heat and some bandages and morphine. A handful of overworked medics did the best they could. These wounded men needed a military hospital. They needed surgeons.

Cole knew better than to ask how much longer they all had to hang on. Without more ammo, without medical supplies, without reinforcements, there would be no holding this position. You didn't have to be a general to know that. Or maybe in this case, everybody seemed to know it except the generals, but that was the Army for you.

As it turned out, Cole didn't need to ask. The lieutenant came looking for Sergeant Weber. He nodded at Cole, but didn't bother to dismiss him. "Sergeant, we've got orders to move out. Get the wounded that can't walk onto the trucks. Tell the men to take all the gear that they can carry. The colonel wants us as far down the road as possible while we still have air cover. We're headed back to Hagaru-ri."

Although the news was inevitable—after all, it was either pull out or get ground to pieces in the next attack—the enormity of it left them more than a little stunned as the news sank in. After pushing so deep into North Korea, the U.S. Army was about to retreat.

CHAPTER NINETEEN

THE RUMBLING of tank engines carried far in the frigid air. Like armored beasts, the tanks seemed right at home in the brutal land- scape. With a clanking of treads and a roar, they started up the frozen road toward the Pungyuri Inlet.

Contrary to what the surrounded soldiers might think, they had not been completely abandoned or forgotten. Riding with the 31st Tank Company, Brigadier General Henry "Hammerin' Hank" Hodes was among those trying to fight their way north to help the stranded troops.

Despite the tanks' appearance of invincibility, so far, the effort to bring the tanks into play on the battlefield had not gone all that well. The tanks under Captain Drake had rushed to the battle zone and arrived by nightfall on November 27th, but their commander had wisely opted for daylight the next day before attempting the narrow road leading north from Hudong-ni.

"Keep your eyes open," Drake had exhorted his men the next day as the three tank platoons moved along the narrow road. His warning was unnecessary because it was more than clear that the road was heavily defended by the Chinese. The Chinese did not have armor or heavy artillery to attack the tanks, but they did have their version of the bazooka. The weapon could fire into the tracks of a tank and disable it. As the tankers quickly discovered, knocking out the lead tank on the narrow road was as good as crippling them all because there was no easy way to get around it.

This was not ideal country for tanks. First of all, there were no clear avenues of fire. Here in the mountains, a tank could only see as far as the next bend in the road. And in this rugged terrain, the road was the only option. Striking out cross country through the steep ravines and mountains was not even possible.

But it was not in the nature of the tankers to sit idly by. If there was even a remote chance of reinforcing their stranded troops, they had to try.

One of those tanks was commanded by Staff Sergeant Paul Roxbury. At age 26, and untested in battle, he was as eager as anyone to take on the enemy.

"Look at this," Roxbury said, pointing out the remains of a medical unit that had tried in vain to bring supplies north. All of their trucks and most of their men had been wiped out by the Chinese. To Roxbury's eyes, the scene looked something like the remains of burned wagons left behind by an Indian attack. "The poor bastards never stood a chance."

Roxbury had to admit that the North Koreans and their Chinese allies knew the terrain, that was for damn sure. The enemy had set up their defenses in and around what was designated as Hill 1221, the tallest and largest of the mountains ringing the Chosin Reservoir. Ironically, the heights had been occupied by Marines until it was necessary for them to withdraw. The Chinese had since taken the high ground, occupied the abandoned defenses, and created a roadblock at a hairpin turn in the road that followed the foot of the mountain. Clearly, the Chinese plan was to use the blockade to prevent U.S. and U.N. forces from retreating—or from anything like this tank column to reinforce them.

Roxbury's tank was the third one back in the column. Up ahead, there was a flash and a trail of blowing smoke that signaled that the Chinese had fired one of their own bazookas at the lead tank.

"They got a direct hit on the lead tank!" Roxbury shouted to his men, practically unable to believe his eyes. The round had knocked the treads off the tank, effectively crippling it. "We have no choice but to go around it."

This proved easier said than done. For starters, the tank just ahead of Roxbury was heading downhill on the frozen road at a good clip. When the tank tried to brake, the result was that it slewed sideways and slid the rest of the way down, coming to rest against the crippled tank. Immediately, the second tank came under small arms fire. Chinese soldiers rushed toward it. Without supporting infantry, the behemoth tanks were largely helpless.

Roxbury looked around for a target to unleash his tank's main gun upon, but saw nothing.

Another Chinese bazooka fired, hitting a tank. This shot had gotten luckier, though, and smoke soon poured from that tank's hatch.

"Back it up!" Roxbury shouted. Again, it was easier said than done. The tracks spun for purchase on the frozen slope. The tank immediately behind Roxbury tried the same maneuver and began to slip off the road and down a steep embankment.

Before long, the order came to withdraw. But for four tanks and twelve men of the unit, the order came too late. There had been a heavy price to pay for trying to relieve the stranded men. And in the end, the rescue attempt hadn't made any difference.

For all their snorting and power, the tanks had not proved up to the task.

Although they were itching to fire on something—anything—Roxbury and his crew had no choice but to withdraw with the other tanks.

Not that the remaining tanks of the 31st were ready to give up. They regrouped and were ordered to try again the next day. Now, they had just a dozen tanks, including the captain's command vehicle. This time, they also had air cover and even a platoon of supporting infantry. The question was, would that platoon be enough?

"I don't know that they'll hold up," Roxbury muttered. "Look at those poor SOBs."

Indeed, the sight of the supporting infantry did not inspire much confidence. Short on men, the captain had rounded up a motley collection of men who did not normally carry a rifle. These were cooks, clerks, and assorted support staff. They all looked grimly determined.

Roxbury had to give them that much. The trouble was that none of them had fired a weapon since basic training. But no one had the luxury anymore of simply being a clerk or a cook. This was turning into one of those battles where a soldier had to be a soldier.

One of them was a clerk named Hood, who still was trying to get used to the feel of a rifle in his hands. That was just about the only thing that he could feel, considering that his feet, ears, cheeks, and fingers were already numb. He was glad when they finally got moving so that he could keep the blood flowing.

Once again, the tank column headed north in hopes of pushing past Hill 1221 and the blockade. Roxbury was reminded of the myth of Sisyphus, the Greek gent who had been doomed for eternity to push a boulder up a hill, only to have it roll back down so that he had to do it all over again. He snorted, thinking that Sisyphus would be a promising nickname for his tank—if they survived the next few hours.

Moving north, the tank column was shadowed by its air support. But they lacked any communication with the Corsairs, which meant that the pilots were just going to have to use their own best judgment. Roxbury had seen what a load of napalm could do, and he wasn't entirely reassured by the planes hovering above.

It didn't take them long to reach the section of road at the base of Hill 1221 where they had run into trouble the day before. The wreckage of the medical unit trucks and the burned hulks of the tanks lost yesterday looked stark against the snow, stinking of burned rubber —and worse.

Once again, the Chinese were waiting for them.

Rifles fired, pinging harmlessly off the steel skin of the tanks. But it was the Chinese bazookas and Bangalore torpedoes that Roxbury was worried about. All that the enemy needed to do was disable one tank to block the road again.

The infantry platoon fanned out along the road, buffering the tank column from attacks by Chinese troops rushing forward with one of those Bangalore torpedo charges. A Corsair swept in, fast and nimble as a sparrow, hammering the hillside with its machine guns.

The trouble was that the pilot had mistaken the figures far below for Chinese troops. Without communication from the ground, he fired at the movement he saw parallel to the road.

"Dear God, no," Roxbury muttered, watching as the heavy slugs mowed down a handful of their own men. Some of those guys didn't even know enough to get down. They died staring up at the sky, never expecting their own planes to shoot at them.

That's when the Chinese opened up on them like they meant it. Machine-gun fire rattled off the tank. An unsettling sound, despite the thick armor skin. Then came the telltale whoosh and smoky plume of a Chinese bazooka fired at the lead tank.

Roxbury thought at first that the tank had come through unscathed. It was still rolling, that was for sure. But the tank was slewing sideways down the road, sliding down the frozen mud. Roxbury cursed. He could see that the right-hand track flapped ineffectively, so that the tank was like a ship without a rudder. The steel beast came to a stop, square in the middle of the road, blocking the rest of the column.

* * *

OUTSIDE, the makeshift infantry platoon of clerks and cooks was busy counter-attacking the Chinese troops closing in on the tanks. At first, Hood had welcomed the chance to actually fight after typing up reports as a company clerk. Now, he felt terrified. He fired his carbine at the Chinese, astonished to be so close to the enemy. Hit by enemy fire, the men on either side of him went down. Hood got off a couple more shots.

The next thing he knew, one of the Chinese threw something at him that proved to be a grenade. Before he could react, Hood was knocked out cold by the blast.

He came to because someone was pounding on his back. He rolled over to find a Chinese soldier bent over him, hitting Hood with his rifle. Either the Chinese soldier had run out of ammunition or his weapon was inoperable in the cold. Lucky for Hood, the soldier didn't seem to have a bayonet for his rifle or hadn't thought of it. From the angry shouts of the soldier, however, it was clear that the man planned to beat Hood to death.

He reached around and grabbed for his own rifle, lying in the dirt and snow nearby. With an effort, he swung the muzzle toward the Chinese soldier and pulled the trigger, killing him.

Then Private Hood rolled to his feet and skedaddled back toward the line of tanks.

* * *

THERE WASN'T much safety to be found among the tanks. Roxbury and the other tankers were astonished when the Chinese attacked the rear tank, trying to knock it out and box them all in. A few bursts from that tank's gun solved the problem temporarily. But the Chinese were far from done. The tank column found itself surrounded.

Another tank was hit, and the crew climbed out to try to make repairs. The Chinese were waiting for them, though, and picked them off. The disabled tank created yet another obstacle on the road.

Roxbury could see that this whole operation was falling apart. He had to admit that the tanks were next to useless on this road, hemmed in by close hills on all sides and unable to use their firepower to any effect. In those hills, the Chinese were dug in too deep to dislodge. He was relieved when the order came to withdraw.

But this would be a fighting retreat.

He opened the hatch so he could guide the tank as it reversed up the icy road—getting the tank turned around wasn't an option. He was surprised to see one of the infantrymen hurrying after them, in danger of being left behind. The poor bastard was bleeding and dragging one leg.

"Climb on!" Roxbury shouted, after ordering his driver to halt.

The soldier got aboard the tank, and they got the hell out of there.

Looking back toward where they had been attacked, he could see that the Chinese had set the disabled tanks on fire. Bodies lay strewn everywhere—some of them wearing Chinese puffy uniforms, and others the olive drab of Americans.

Most of the infantrymen who had been pressed into service were now dead, brave but unfortunate bastards that they were. They had lost two more tanks. The Chinese hadn't budged. Nobody was going to the rescue of the stranded troops.

What a snafu, Roxbury thought, only too glad to get the hell out of there while they still could.

CHAPTER TWENTY

MILES TO THE NORTH, unaware of the efforts of the tank column to come to their aid, the soldiers prepared to withdraw. Nobody was calling it a retreat. When the kid called it that, he was quickly corrected.

"So we're retreating?" the kid asked.

"Don't you know anything, kid? It's bad luck to call it that. It ain't a retreat," Pomeroy informed him. "It's what you'd call a tactical withdrawal."

Cole grinned. "You know what, New Jersey? You ought to be an officer," Cole told him. "Nobody but an officer could find a pretty way of saying we're running off like a dog with his tail between his legs."

"Yeah, and if that dog has got any sense he'll keep on running. If the Chinese catch him, they might eat him. They're barbarians."

Cole snorted. "Hell, I've eaten worse than that. What would you call me?"

Pomeroy gave him a look, but seemed to know better than to ask what could be worse than eating a dog.

Anyhow, they were too busy to get into the finer culinary points. The whole camp was in a rush to get packed up and on the road out of this godforsaken place. There wasn't a soldier there who wasn't eager to get out of there before nightfall, when it was likely that the Chinese would return.

Slowly, it had dawned on many of the Americans that there was a very real possibility of becoming prisoners of the Chinese. Surrounded, cut off, the GIs were facing that uncomfortable thought. It was a little less likely that they would fight to the last man. Each man struggled with the disbelief that this was actually happening. By tomorrow he might be dead. By tomorrow, he might be a POW.

Cole had seen mass surrenders take place in the last war, with the Germans. Often, the way it happened had a kind of snowball effect. Two or three men would give up, and then entire squads, and finally you had a whole unit waving a white flag—especially at the end of the war when it made a whole lot more sense to surrender to the Americans or British, rather than to the oncoming Russian hordes. Germans who surrendered to the Russians did not fare well. Many had been marched deep into Russia, never to return. Would the Americans meet the same fate if they surrendered?

Nearby, some of the men were yammering about it. Cole didn't like to hear the word "surrender" openly discussed because he thought it opened the door to the wrong way of thinking.

Leaning in to hear more, the kid was all ears. He turned to Cole and said, "Those guys are talking about surrendering."

"I'm not gonna lie. The Chinese have our nuts in a vise."

"You think the Chinese would feed us?" the kid asked. "Maybe give us someplace to warm up?"

"Them Chinese are worse off than us," Cole said. "It ain't like they got a luxury hotel over the next hill. These fools who think surrendering is a good idea are making one hell of a mistake."

"I guess you're right." The kid nodded, looking dejected. He had a blanket over his shoulders, but he was still shivering. Cole thought that maybe it wasn't that the kid was intent on surrendering, but that like the others, he needed some nugget of hope that this wasn't the end of the line.

Cole relented. He took the younger man by the shoulders and gave him a hard stare with his flinty eyes. "Look kid, if it comes down to it and you've got no choice but to surrender, you do it. And then you survive. You do whatever it takes to get home again. Understand?"

The kid nodded.

Cole turned to Pomeroy. "How are those feet, New Jersey? We can try to find you some room on one of the trucks."

"Hell no. Save the trucks for the wounded."

"Wounded? You already got shot once and your feet are frozen."

"I'll make it out of here on my own two feet, one way or another. Don't you worry about me."

Cole nodded. He wasn't going to argue with Pomeroy. Hell, he wouldn't have wanted to ride in the trucks, either.

If the thought of becoming POWs made the GIs uneasy, it downright terrified the ROK soldiers fighting alongside them. In their case, capture likely meant certain death. The Americans had at least some chance of being made POWs and not shot outright if they were captured. You didn't have to be Dean Acheson to see that there was some political advantage to having captured U.S. forces as pawns. But nobody needed the ROKs as pawns, which meant that they would likely be shot out of hand as traitors.

"Better get something to eat," Cole said to Pomeroy and Tommy. "There's no telling when we'll have another chance once we're on the move."

"I could use a T-bone steak and maybe a baked potato with butter," Pomeroy said. "How about you, Kid?"

"S—s-ure, sounds good," he stammered through blue lips.

"I reckon you'll have to settle for a can of half froze rations," Cole said. "But it's better than nothing."

On that much, they could agree. The three of them settled back into the hole, out of the wind, and shoveled down the cold, congealed food. Still, it wasn't enough. In these temperatures, their bodies burned calories like a hot rod guzzles gas. When they were done, they tossed away the empty cans and got to work.

Quickly, they rolled up and stowed their sleeping bags on one of the trucks designated for that purpose. There wasn't much else to carry, aside from their weapons, a few spare rounds of ammo, a couple of grenades, and a trenching tool. They carried their canteens inside their coats to keep them from freezing.

Over the last two days, Colonel McLean had the good sense to order that the trucks be run every few hours, in order to keep the batteries from draining in the cold. The tanks were topped off with the last of the gasoline, and the convoy would be ready to move out once the trucks were loaded.

Cole set aside his rifle and helped to load the wounded into the trucks. There was hardly enough space for them all, so that the stretchers had to be stacked one on top of the other, like lumber. There weren't even enough stretchers, so some of the wounded were just bundled up into blankets. Most of these men were grievously wounded, some even shot several times. A few had managed to survive being bayoneted by the Chinese. Others had lost limbs to grenades or mortars. These last men had tourniquets made of parachute strapping or even belts holding in their life's blood.

It was a miracle that some of them had survived, given their grievous wounds, but they had the cold to thank for that. The frigid temperatures had served to cauterize their wounds. Most suffered in silence, or at the most, uttered a few curses. A few of the lucky ones actually slept or remained unconscious. Cole felt sorry for the poor bastards, every last one of them.

They faced a truly uncomfortable trip. The back of the trucks, though covered with canvas, had no heaters. Each jolt of the rugged road sent fresh agony through this shattered cargo.

The medics trying to tend them looked exhausted. Most of the medics hadn't slept in two days—not since the first attack. Some were injured themselves, either from the fighting or from frostbite. They had to treat an overwhelming number of wounded with very limited supplies. Every last one of the medics was a goddamn hero in Cole's book.

While the wounded had it rough, these men were far more fortunate than those in the last couple of trucks being loaded. These were the dead. Their frozen bodies were stuffed into the backs of trucks. With the ground too frozen to bury them, the decision had been made to bring the dead along. There was no way to load the bodies neatly, so that in the end the stray arms and legs stuck out the back, creating a macabre cargo of tangled, frozen limbs.

All available supplies also were loaded onto the trucks. What couldn't fit into the trucks was being stacked nearby. This included the wall tents and some of the gear left behind by the wounded. Also being discarded were the useless rounds in the wrong caliber, left from the disastrous air drop that seemed to be all the help that they were going to get.

"Burn it," Sergeant Weber barked. "Burn it all!"

Somebody doused the piles with diesel fuel and tossed in a match. Flames began to reach upward, sending black smoke high into the mountain air. Cole figured that it wouldn't take long for the Chinese to figure out what was happening, once they saw that smoke. Only a retreating force would burn their gear.

The question was, would the enemy simply let them march out of there? Cole thought it seemed unlikely. He made sure that the action of his rifle was working in the cold before slipping it over his shoulder.

In the distance, he saw the two officers, Colonel McLean and Lieutenant Colonel Don Faith. Both carried weapons, which was unusual in the colonel's case because he was known for carrying a cane most of the time. The weapons that the officers now held signaled that this might very well be a fighting retreat. Cole took some reassurance from the sight, however, knowing that both men were capable officers. If anyone could get them out of this mess, it was these two men.

No orders came down to move out. The first truck at the head of the convoy simply began driving forward, and the rest slowly followed.

"Let's move out!" the lieutenant shouted, unnecessarily. "No stragglers!"

"Listen to him," Pomeroy muttered. "He ought to save his breath. Nobody plans on being the last man out, that's for damn sure."

Pomeroy limped along with the others, a blanket draped over his shoulders. The kid followed along behind. There was no real marching order, with squads and groups moving between or alongside the creeping trucks. The pace was excruciatingly slow, with the trucks never getting out of first gear. It didn't help that the GIs knew the whole goddamn Chinese army was right behind them. This wasn't exactly a time for slow going, but what choice was there other than abandoning the wounded? Nobody was doing that.

Cole walked off to one side, watching for movement beyond the roadside. The American column was strung out for nearly a mile along the narrow road. If the Chinese wanted to hit them now, they were sitting ducks. Calling this a road was something of a misnomer because this was just a narrow lane, covered in snow, icy in patches, and pock-marked with ruts. The road took its time, meandering as it went.

Sergeant Weber wandered over beside him. "Keep an eye out, Cole. I know that you must be good with that rifle, whether you admit it or not, and you might get a chance to use it before the day is out."

Cole's sharp eyes caught movement on the hills bordering the road. He stared, trying to make sense of what he had seen. Chinese troops were moving into position to pour harassing fire down on them from the hills, or maybe even attempt to cut them off from Hagaru-ri. "You know what? I reckon I will get that chance," Cole said.

They made it maybe an hour before the first Chinese attack.

CHAPTER TWENTY-ONE

As GUNFIRE PEPPERED THE COLUMN, Cole scanned the hills, looking for targets. The nature of this landscape made holding the high ground impossible for the Americans and their allies. Hills marched away from both sides of the road and they could clearly see Chinese troops covering them.

The only blessing was that the Chinese did not seem to possess artillery. If that had been the case, then the U.N. column would have been obliterated. Still, the Chinese were not prevented from firing down from the hills. From time to time, squads of the enemy approached to attack the column with grenades, always targeting the trucks.

Officers who were students of history couldn't help but think of the punishing march made by the British from Lexington and Concord back to Boston. Enraged by the sight of enemy soldiers on their soil, the colonials had pestered the Redcoats with hit-and-run attacks. Now, the tables had turned and it was these Americans who were the enemy on someone else's home turf. And yet, they were not the soldiers of any king, but the soldiers of democracy and freedom. Too bad the Communists didn't see it that way.

For soldiers who were already exhausted, being on constant guard against enemy attack was pushing them beyond the limits of their endurance. Bleary eyed, every bush or boulder became an enemy soldier. It was only their lack of ammunition that kept them from shooting up the countryside.

"They're going to pick us off one by one," Pomeroy remarked. "I overheard one of the officers say it's fourteen miles to Hagaru-ri. Might as well be a hundred."

"Just keep your eyes open," Cole said. "You see one of them bastards in a puffy coat, you shoot him. That ought to make them think twice about attacking us."

Pomeroy gave Cole a look. "I can tell you've done this before."

"What?"

"Fight."

"Yeah. I had me a little experience in the last war."

The road began to curve and descend toward the Pungyuri River. If there was ever a place for an ambush, Cole thought, this was it. The river was crossed by a narrow bridge that had been previously reinforced by Army engineers when the unit had been heading north. Now that they were retreating, it was something of a small miracle that the bridge was still intact. The bridge itself was close to the surface of the water. Ice gripped the rocky edges of the waterway, but at the center of the river the water ran free—despite the cold, there was simply too much current for the water to freeze over.

"I sure as hell wouldn't want to fall in there," Pomeroy said. "Can you swim?"

Cole shook his head. He hated any kind of water, having almost drowned once in a mountain stream when trapping as a boy. It was more than he wanted to explain to Pomeroy right now, but he had to admit to himself that the sight of that cold, dark current made him shudder. "Pomeroy, how much gear do you have on? How long do you reckon anyone could swim in that current?"

"I guess you're right."

As they neared the bridge, a squad of soldiers moved forward to scout the approach and make sure that an ambush had not been set. The soldiers set up a perimeter along both sides of the bridge, hunkering down on the rocky shore.

Cole was surprised to see a column of soldiers appear on the far side of the river and begin advancing across the bridge. These troops were clearly on the march, not rushing toward a fight. Their weapons were slung over their shoulders. They did not appear to be wearing the tell-tale quilted winter uniforms. In fact, they wore olive drab like the U.N. troops. But Cole's sharp eyes picked out the fact that something wasn't quite right. Hell, they just didn't *move* like Americans.

He wasn't the only one to spot the approaching soldiers. Almost immediately, the squad along the river bank began to open fire. Some of the advancing soldiers were hit and fell into the river, only to be swept away in the icy current. It was a nightmarish sight and terrified screams reached their ears.

"Stop!"

Even over the shooting, they could hear someone yelling urgently. A figure ran onto the bridge from the American side, waving his cane over his head. Immediately, the fire on the American side slackened as his troops recognized their commanding officer, Colonel MacLean. He shouted again: "Hold your fire! Those are my boys!"

Out on the bridge, the colonel ran toward the approaching troops. To the colonel, it seemed clear that these were reinforcements sent from Hagaru-ri. Help had finally come for his battered troops. Also, it meant that the road ahead must be clear if the reinforcements had made it through.

"I'll be damned," Pomeroy muttered. "Looks like we weren't forgotten, after all."

Recognizing that help had arrived, some of the soldiers around Cole and Pomeroy began to whoop. Ten minutes ago, they had been mired in despair. Now, they at least had some hope of getting the hell out of this place in one piece.

But Cole saw that something was wrong. Although the firing from their own side of the crossing had stopped when the colonel ran out onto the bridge, the newly arrived troops were quickly unshouldering their rifles and shouting. Some of the other troops opened fire, their rifle reports making sharp cracks in the cold air.

The colonel staggered and dropped his cane. He was hit again and went to his knees. More shots were fired. He fell to the deck of the bridge, struggling to get up.

Now, a handful of the soldiers on the bridge were running toward the fallen colonel. Too late, Cole and the others realized what was happening. These were not reinforcements. These were simply Chinese or maybe North Korean troops without their winter uniforms. Clearly, they had been taken by complete surprise at the sight of an American officer running at them, waving a cane, but the surprise had not lasted for long.

Cole's rifle was already up. He put his sights on the soldier closest to the fallen colonel and fired. The man went down. Other soldiers were doing the same, although the enemy troops were now so close that it seemed an even chance that their shots were just as likely to hit the colonel. Seeing the situation, some officers and sergeants shouted for the shooting to stop, adding to the confusion.

Out on the bridge, the enemy soldiers had reached the wounded colonel and were dragging him back to their side of the river. Helplessly, his own troops watched as their colonel was taken prisoner. Holding the colonel awkwardly by the coat and his arms and legs, enemy soldiers half-carried, half-dragged him off the bridge and hustled away with their prize. At that point, however, it was hard to tell if the limp figure was even alive.

The whole episode had taken less than a minute, but it left the Americans stunned and dumbfounded. The colonel had been one of the good ones. He knew what he was doing, which was more than they could say for a lot of officers.

They couldn't know it at the time, but their colonel would be the highest-ranking U.S. officer to be captured in the entire war.

Once the colonel was out of sight, it was open season on the enemy troops still on the bridge. Someone opened up with a BAR, and corpses soon covered the bridge. More fell into the river. Some of those men hadn't even been hit, but were forced off the bridge in the turmoil, only to drown in the swift, icy current.

Wanting to save his ammunition, Cole lowered his rifle and let the BAR do its deadly work. The bridge was soon clear of enemy soldiers, and the first trucks of the convoy rolled across it. If they were lucky,

the column would get across before the enemy organized a coun-
terattack.

"It's a hell of a thing," Pomeroy said, as they waited their turn to
cross the bridge. "If they got the colonel like that, those sons of
bitches can get anybody."

"Hell of a thing," Cole agreed, trying not to think too much about
the last glimpse he'd seen of the colonel, being hauled away like a
carcass being dragged by a pack of wolves. He shook his head to clear
that vision. "Like I said, keep your eyes open."

* * *

EARLIER THAT MORNING, Chen had rejoiced with the other Chinese
troops when they saw that the enemy was leaving. They watched with
fascination as the enemy soldiers loaded their trucks with supplies,
then their wounded, and even their dead. Chen was puzzled about the
dead being taken away. He thought it was macabre and strange. Let the
dead rest in peace. He had seen enough of war that he knew it made
very little difference to the dead where they lay. Their spirits had
moved on to join their ancestors.

Not only that, but when it came to the imperialist invaders, he
would have preferred to see their bones picked clean and bleached
where they had fallen.

Finally, the enemy convoy began to move, but not before setting
fire to what they could not carry. Again, it made no sense to Chen.
Why carry away the dead but leave supplies that the living could use?
With thinking like that, perhaps it was no surprise that the Americans
had been defeated.

But letting the Americans escape was not enough. They must
punish them. The officers gave orders, sending squads of men racing
into the hills to cut off the Americans. Chen and his comrades were
eager for this task. A further number of troops were sent to simply
attack the rear of the American convoy. What the Americans could
not know was that there was no open road ahead of them, either. More
soldiers already waited for them, blocking the road.

Chen attached himself to a small squad that ran into the hills.

Their orders were to move parallel to the column and attack it. Although the enemy was already some distance ahead, that mattered little to Chen and his comrades, who ran like deer through the snow and brush. The promise of revenge made them fleet.

Yet the enemy was not entirely toothless. One of the soldiers pointed at the sky and shouted, "Plane!"

The man had good hearing, but Chen had sharp eyes. "It is coming from the South!" he warned them.

Out in the open, the men scattered, trying to hide in the brush or even to cower among the rocks and boulders.

The Corsair came in low, its engine roaring. Had the pilot spotted them?

Chen and the others held their breath. They knew all too well what the enemy bomb and napalm could do.

With a roar, the plane swept overhead and was gone.

Either the pilot hadn't spotted them, after all, or he simply hadn't wanted to bother with a handful of men and was looking for a bigger target.

Dusting the snow off themselves, they gave a nervous look at the sky, and ran on.

They reached a hill that overlooked the road and looked down at the plodding enemy column, each of the Chinese soldiers panting as they caught their breath. There was no need for orders. He and the others started moving down the hill, approaching the column.

By now, Chen thought, he and his comrades must surely be in plain sight of the enemy. But the Americans ignored them, heads down, intent only on the road. They moved so close that they could plainly see the pale, ugly, haggard faces of the enemy.

"Now, Comrades!" Chen said.

Their orders were to attack the trucks. To fire directly into them. To target the drivers. Chen knew that the trucks carried the enemy wounded. Helpless men. But it did not matter. He and the others had come to harass the enemy. The enemy would be shown no mercy, not even the wounded.

Chen took aim at the canvas sides of a truck and fired. Worked the bolt. Fired again. And again. He was so close that he could see the actual holes that his bullets punched through the fabric. Inside the truck, he could hear the agonized cries of the wounded. Ignoring them, he continued to fire.

* * *

SINCE CROSSING THE BRIDGE, hit and run attacks had been happening all around Cole and the others. This time, the Chinese were attacking a truck right in front of them.

"The sons of bitches are shooting into the trucks!" someone shouted.

Horrified, they realized that the Chinese were targeting the wounded. From inside the trucks, they could hear the screams of help-less men as bullets found them. A Chinese soldier ran onto the road, ignoring Cole and the others. He dashed right to the back of another truck and tossed something inside.

"Grenade!" someone screamed.

The Chinese soldier threw himself flat, but it didn't do him any good because Cole shot him, leaving him writhing on the ground. He didn't bother to finish him off.

Then the grenade detonated, exploding with a flash that instantly incinerated the canvas sides. Some men spilled out, their clothes on fire. Others screamed as they burned in their stretchers. The lucky ones had died instantly. Now, the fire was spreading to the rest of the truck, the tires catching, flames flaring from under the hood.

At the side of the road, the Chinese advanced, shooting at any of the wounded clawing their way out of the burning truck. The stunned, disorganized soldiers were torn between attacking the Chinese and helping the wounded escape the onslaught.

It was too much to watch. With a roar of rage, a soldier near Cole rushed at the Chinese, firing an M-1 carbine from the hip as he ran.

"Come on!" Pomeroy cried, and likewise ran at the enemy, firing. The kid followed at his heels, screaming what sounded like an Indian war cry. Two ROK soldiers joined in.

Startled by the ferocity of the rushing soldiers, the Chinese fell back. They scattered and ran deeper into the roadside brush. After all, their intent had been to harass the Americans, not stand and fight.

Cole chased after the others, although he had not fired a shot during the pursuit. Ahead of him, he watched with concern as his buddies ran deeper into the brush. "Come back!" he shouted, but nobody was listening.

Muttering a curse, he ran after them. Cole knew that this entire countryside was crawling with enemy soldiers. If those guys didn't watch it, they were going to run smack dab into the whole damn Chinese army.

CHAPTER TWENTY-TWO

A MAD RAGE overtook the men chasing the Chinese soldiers. All the anger and pent-up fear of the last few days added wings to their feet. They ran after the fleeing attackers like hounds hunting rabbits. The Chinese obliged them by running for their lives, rather than staying to fight.

"Those sons of bitches are getting away!" somebody shouted, urging the others on.

Even Pomeroy managed to join the chase, running with an awkward lope because of his frostbitten feet, carried along by adrenalin, pausing now and then to fire his carbine at the retreating Chinese. Along with Cole, Pomeroy, and Tommy, three other soldiers from their squad had joined the chase, intent on revenge.

Cole was fairly certain that a couple of those guys were ROK. The South Koreans hadn't been great soldiers, being more than happy to let the Americans do the lion's share of fighting, but now desperation was making them ferocious. They finally understood that it was kill or be killed on the road to Hagaru-ri.

Listening to their enraged shouts, Cole was beginning to think that maybe he had underestimated the ROK soldiers up until now.

All the pent-up frustrations of the past few days propelled the

American and ROK soldiers across the snowy landscape. Branches tore at their uniforms and rocks threatened to trip them. They lost their footing in the snow and ice, but they didn't slow down.

Only Cole hung back. There would be plenty of other enemy soldiers to deal with before the day was through. "Hold up!" he shouted, trying to rein in the others. "Let 'em go!"

Nobody was listening. He chased the others up the side of a hill, then at the crest he stopped to glance back at the road, where the column of trucks and soldiers was almost out of sight through the scrub brush. The column moved at a snail's pace, but Cole worried that they might get left behind, nonetheless.

From his vantage point, he could see now that it had been the perfect location for an ambush. Come to think of it, this *entire* countryside was the perfect place for an ambush.

The Chinese hadn't even targeted the soldiers on foot or the truck drivers. Instead, they had blatantly shot into the canvas sides of the trucks, knowing full well that the trucks carried wounded men. From a war-fighting standpoint, it didn't make much sense to shoot men who had already been shot. However, the Chinese seemed to want to send a message that they could attack the wounded, and there wasn't a damn thing that the American soldiers could do about it.

Cole was as mad as the rest, but he didn't see the sense of running right into a larger unit. It was a classic decoy tactic. He had seen coyotes do the same thing. A single coyote would come onto a farm and lure a dog into chasing it. A coyote on its own was no match for most dogs, being much smaller. But once the dog was far enough from the farm, the rest of the coyote pack would descend. Overwhelmed from all sides, the dog didn't have a chance.

"Ya'll come back!" Cole shouted, but no one paid him any mind. "New Jersey! Kid! Git yer asses back here!"

All that he could see was the backs of the other soldiers, pushing deeper into the scrub brush. He considered firing a shot into the air to get their attention, but he might need that bullet later.

"Dang fools," he muttered, scrambling down the other side of the hill. The snow-covered rocks and shale threatened to send him sprawling, but he managed to keep his balance. He looked behind him again, but now the American convoy was hidden from view.

Up ahead, he heard a sudden burst of fire, then shouting. More shots followed as the Americans returned fire. Their M-1 rifles had a distinctive crack that sounded different from the Chinese weapons.

Cole hurried to catch up, worried that the others had finally run into the main body of Chinese soldiers. But there didn't seem to be enough shooting for that. Maybe the Chinese that they'd been chasing had finally turned to fight.

Cole knew better than to go charging into the middle of the firefight. He had lost sight of the others; if he ran up to them they might mistake him for an enemy. Cole decided to circle wide around the fight and see if he could come at the enemy from the flank.

He swung up another hill, keeping to the high ground. That would give him a vantage point to come at the enemy from above.

Silently, he cursed the fact that he had just two full clips for the M-1. He had to make each bullet count.

Cole kept to the low brush, picking his way quietly through the tangled branches. He was beyond quiet, despite his hurry, moving with no more sound than the snow had made sifting down the night before. This was a skill that he had mastered in the mountains as a boy. There was quiet, and then there was Cole.

Below and to his left, the firing grew in intensity. The Chinese were making it plenty hot for the other guys, that was for sure. Like Cole, they were also short on ammo. If more Chinese troops appeared, they would be in big trouble.

Finally, Cole emerged through a break in the brush where he could look down and get a glimpse of the enemy soldiers firing on the Americans. There were a lot more Chinese than they had seen running from the road. Sure enough, the Americans had run smack-dab into a larger unit. Unfortunately, they also seemed to have plenty of bullets.

Cole decided to even the odds. He lay down on his belly in the snow. One thing that the Chinese had figured out that the Americans hadn't was camouflage. Against the snowy backdrop, the quilted cotton uniforms that the Chinese wore blended in all too well. Some of the enemy also wore white snow capes or ponchos—simple but effective for concealment. Cole kicked himself for not borrowing a cape from one of the dead Chinese.

To stay hidden, he kept among the tangled scrub brush, where his olive drab coat blended in somewhat. Then he took aim at the Chinese below. He missed having a telescopic sight, but at this range he saw his targets clearly in the iron sights of the Garand. Shooting downhill, he aimed a little low. When he squeezed the trigger, his first target went down. He moved his rifle and picked out the next soldier.

Considering that they were deep in Indian Country, the thought of who might be sneaking up behind him made the hairs stand up on the back of his neck. He forced the unnerving thought from his mind and focused on the enemy targets. Without a spotter, he would just have to trust his ears and his natural sixth sense, the Critter. So far, it had kept him alive.

He fired again, and again, making each shot count. He heard the distinctive *ping* of the empty clip sailing away and quickly loaded his final clip but held his fire. The Chinese had stopped firing. Confronted by the determination of the Americans and now a sniper on their flank, the Chinese appeared to be falling back.

Cole crept down toward where the Americans had been making their stand.

"It's Cole," he said as loud as he dared, with the Chinese so close. "I'm coming in. Don't shoot my ass."

"Cole, where the hell you been?"

"Saving your sorry asses, that's where."

Sheltering in a shallow ravine, Cole found the other men who had given chase. Now that their initial rage at the Chinese had worn off, they looked as if they might be regretting their choices. Alone and low on ammo, for all they knew they had been cut off from the American column on the road. Cole wondered how far had they run chasing these bastards? Looking around at the bleak, empty landscape, the answer was clear enough. Too far.

He was glad to see that Pomeroy and the kid were OK. He couldn't say the same for the others. One of the ROK soldiers was dead, surrounded by gore-soaked snow. The surviving ROK soldier was busy going through the dead man's pockets—whether to loot them or just collect his valuables for his family, it was hard to say. Cole wasn't curious enough to ask. The other American had been hit in the leg, and he was clumsily trying to bandage it himself.

"Here, let me do that," Cole muttered with a grunt. Setting his rifle nearby, he bent down to inspect the leg. "Lucky for you, it looks like the bullet went through the meat of your calf. Once we get the bleeding stopped, you should be able to walk on it."

"It's gonna be a long walk back to the road," the soldier said, gritting his teeth as Cole set to work wrapping the leg tightly.

"It's an even longer walk back to Shanghai," Cole said. It was the only Chinese city that he could think of, although he was pretty sure that had more to do with sailors than soldiers. "Let's hope to hell that we can get back to the main column before these Chinese come back with a few of their friends."

He bent low to pull the last of the bandage tightly. Pomeroy and the kid had been whispering together about something, and he was dimly aware that they had fallen silent.

Looking up, he saw a soldier of Asian appearance looking down at them from the top of the ravine, holding a submachine gun. He thought at first that it was the South Korean. But how the hell had he gotten up there, and where had he gotten that submachine gun?

"Watch where you point that thing, goddammit," Cole said.

The soldier scowled at Cole but didn't avert the muzzle of the submachine gun. Frustrated, Cole did what any English-speaking American did when confronted by someone who didn't understand him. He repeated himself, shouting it this time. "I said, watch where you point that thing!"

When the soldier didn't oblige, Cole just shook his head in disgust. He reached for his rifle, thinking that he would pop his head over the rim of the ravine to see if the Chinese had returned.

Pomeroy spoke urgently. "Hillbilly, you'd better drop that rifle real quick. We've surrendered."

Cole shot a look at Pomeroy, who crouched with his hands over his head. The kid was doing the same. To his dismay, he saw that the ROK soldier was down in the ravine with them, his hands raised—which meant he *wasn't* the guy holding the submachine gun. Cole looked up again and saw more soldiers appear at the edge of the ravine, pointing down at them with weapons.

Cole took a closer look at the soldiers standing above them. They wore those odd-looking quilted uniforms. One of them had on a snow cape.

The soldiers were Chinese.

Slowly, Cole put down the rifle and raised his hands over his head.

I might not get home for Christmas, after all, he was thinking.

CHAPTER TWENTY-THREE

HELD AT GUNPOINT, Cole and the others looked at each other apprehensively. They were all down in a shallow ravine, sheltered somewhat from the incessant wind. However, the ravine also made a natural stockade, with no easy means of escape. For the enemy, it would be like shooting fish in a barrel.

If the enemy had wanted to kill them, they would have done it out of hand. The question was, now what?

He suspected that it was the first time that any of them had seen the soldiers of the other side up close—living soldiers, in any case. These enemy soldiers could not be dismissed as little Asian men, as so many of the American troops were wanted to perceive the enemy. They were just as tall and heavy as the Americans. They did smell kind of bad, though, something that went beyond the usual soldier stink of grime and cordite. Kind of like boiled onions and garlic, Cole thought.

Must be what they ate. He wondered how the Americans must smell to their captors. Maybe like old hamburgers?

"Cole?" the kid asked, looking at him.

"Best be quiet, kid."

That exchange prompted a stream of angry words from their captors. Cole raised his hands higher, not sure what else to do.

Cole took stock of who else was being held with him. There was Pomeroy with his frostbitten feet, along with the kid, who now looked even more scared than he had the first night, when screaming hordes of the enemy had descended upon them. There was a guy whose name he thought was Thompson, who had been wounded slightly in the leg during the earlier firefight. He was the guy that Cole had been patching up when they were captured. Tall and gangly, Thompson kept swallowing nervously so that his Adam's apple bobbed up and down.

None of them seemed to have a plan up his sleeve for escaping. At the moment, neither did Cole.

Finally, there was the surviving ROK soldier. The South Korean's face had gone blank, as if accepting his fate. The faces of their captors were equally hard to read. He had to hand it to these Chinese and the Koreans from both sides—they would have made great poker players.

Cole counted just six captors, but they were all armed, with their rifles never wavering from their prisoners. A couple of their captors wore slightly different uniforms from the others. North Koreans? The other four were clearly Chinese.

One in particular stood out. He was older than the others, for starters. He had a look about him of an old campaigner who had seen everything. He wore a distinctive ushanka hat that appeared to be trimmed with fur. For all that Cole knew, it could have been wolf fur. There was a hardness about the man that Cole recognized—looking into that face, Cole might have been looking into a mirror. What stood out most of all was that this soldier carried a rifle with a telescopic sight. Here was a Chinese sniper.

Momentarily, the sniper locked eyes with Cole. If he saw any of the same qualities in Cole, it did not register on his face. His eyes then flicked to the Confederate flag painted on Cole's helmet and stared at it in curiosity, probably wondering if it was some kind of unit designation.

Cole noticed that the others stood apart from this man, which wasn't surprising. Snipers weren't all that popular with anybody, even their own troops, who treated them with some suspicion. An opposing enemy's view of snipers was less ambivalent. They were hated. Had

Cole been captured with a sniper rifle, he probably wouldn't still be breathing.

Cole studied the Chinese sniper's rifle with professional interest. It appeared to be a Mosin-Nagant. A Russian rifle, then. Not so different from what he had seen enemy snipers carry in the last war. The Chinese appeared to be getting plenty of help from their Russian friends. Judging by the hard look of that Chinese sniper, he was probably a good shot with that rifle. Those eyes had likely been the last ones to see more than a few American boys alive.

Although Cole had sworn off being a sniper, he suddenly itched to have his hands around his old Springfield rifle once more. He might teach this hard-looking fellow a trick or two and take him down a notch. But it was too late for that now. Cole had missed his chance. He was totally at the mercy of these Chinese.

One of the enemy soldiers started shouting orders at his comrades. Apparently, the others didn't agree, because a kind of argument broke out. The disagreement seemed to be between the Chinese and the two North Koreans—who kept gesturing at the captives with their rifles, as if suggesting that shooting them was still an option on the table. Only the sniper stood by quietly, his eyes—and his rifle—trained on the captives.

The soldiers seemed to reach some agreement. Quickly, they moved to tie the captives' hands behind their back. They only had some rather thick rope for that purpose, and in the winter air, with their cold fingers, the rope proved hard to knot properly. It was more of a gesture, it seemed, to keep the North Koreans happy.

When it was Cole's turn, he feigned cooperation and then strained with all his might against the rope as it was tied, ensuring that the binding wasn't very tight. The result was that the thick rope looked impressive but was relatively loose, although they cut cruelly into Cole's wrists. Not that the binding mattered much because there didn't seem to be much chance of overpowering their captors, who kept their distance.

Next, Cole and the others were searched. Their weapons had already been taken, but now they were relieved of the few clips of spare ammunition that they possessed. Cole hated the thought that the ammo and their rifles might now be used against U.N. forces. From what he had seen so far, the Chinese scavenged whatever weapons they could.

One of the Chinese appeared delighted to find Pomeroy's cigarettes.

"Smoke up," Pomeroy muttered. "I hope you cough to death."

But it was Cole's Bowie knife that created the most excitement. They gathered around to study the Damascus steel blade with admiration. Damn, but Cole hated to see them get ahold of that knife. His late friend Hollis had made it for him and Cole had carried it across most of Europe.

There was nothing he could do about them taking that knife, though. It took a sharp word or two from the sniper to get the soldiers focused again on the task at hand. They took the bayonets off the others.

Another argument broke out, this one seemingly about who got to keep Cole's knife. Again, the Chinese sniper spoke a sharp word or two, and the soldier who had taken it off Cole reluctantly handed it over to the sniper.

All that Cole could do was glare at him. The son of a bitch had taken his knife. The Chinese sniper sneered back in what seemed to be his first display of emotion. He tucked the Bowie knife into his belt.

Satisfied that their prisoners were subdued and disarmed, the Chinese motioned for them to climb out of the ravine. Evidently, it was time to get a move on. Cole could see that Tommy wanted to ask him again what was happening, but Cole shook his head at him. There was no sense in provoking their captors. He glanced at Pomeroy, saw his pained expression as they started walking. His frostbitten feet must hurt like hell, but Pomeroy didn't make a sound.

They headed north, most likely toward the larger body of Chinese troops. There was no cover aside from the thickets of brush and the rocky outcroppings. The whole countryside appeared arid and desolate, especially in winter. They didn't seem to be following any sort of trail, but were striking out cross country, likely taking what their captors saw as the shortest route back to the main body of Chinese troops. The route might be faster, but they were taking a chance with those planes roaming overhead. Cole didn't want to get barbecued alive with a load of napalm.

Cole tried not to think too much about what might await them there. Definitely interrogation, maybe even torture. If they were taken as far as the main Chinese army, there would be no escape. Their only hope was to get away while they still had some chance of returning to the retreating column on the road. But how?

The Chinese seemed worried about that same possibility, keeping a close eye on their captives. The captives were forced to walk in a single file, with the kid leading the way. Next came the ROK soldier and Thompson, followed by Pomeroy and Cole. The Chinese urged them on with angry commands that cracked like whips, even if Cole couldn't understand a single word.

Off in the distance, he heard a couple of planes. Because they had yet to see a single Chinese plane, these must surely be American aircraft. The Chinese heard them, too, and looked nervously in that direction. But the planes were too far off to be any threat to the Chinese, or to be any help to the captives. Still, the Chinese urged them on with sharp words in hope of covering the open ground without being seen.

They set a fast pace. Cole could see that the soldier named Thompson was having a hard time keeping up. His leg still bled from the wound that he had received, and he soon began dragging it and stumbling. Pain was etched clearly in the man's face, but the nearest Chinese soldier hit him cruelly in the ribs with a butt of a rifle, urging him on. Cole glanced at Pomeroy, who was managing to keep up so far.

Behind his back, Cole kept moving his hands, working to loosen the rope binding his wrists even more. If he could just get his hands free, he might have some kind of chance of escape. He sure as hell wouldn't get very far with his hands tied. He would have to make a move soon—each step was carrying them closer to the main Chinese force, from which there would be no hope of escape.

CHAPTER TWENTY-FOUR

A FEW STEPS ahead of Cole, the wounded soldier stumbled yet again. The man was obviously in a lot of pain and was going to be slowing them down. They were wading through drifted snow past their knees, and Thompson was leaving a bloody trail behind. It was a wonder that the man was still on his feet.

However, the Chinese sniper appeared to be losing patience with the wounded man. The sniper shouted and shoved the man roughly. Once again, the man stumbled. Instead of waiting for him to get to his feet, the sniper raised his rifle and shot him in the head. There had been no warning. One moment, the soldier was struggling through the snow. The next moment, a spray of gore that had once been the man's brains painted the snow. His body twitched a few times and lay still.

Horrified, the kid froze and stared at the mangled body. The Chinese were not interested in stopping, however. They shouted angrily and gave Tommy a vicious shove.

"*Yídòng tā!*"

The message needed no translation: *Keep moving!* The kid was smart enough to do just that, for which Cole was grateful. These soldiers were murderous bastards. In the deep snow, the surviving captives were forced to step over the dead man's body in order to stay on the trail carved by the two Chinese soldiers in the lead. Cole had seen a few cold-blooded killings in his time, and was even guilty of a few himself, but what he had just witnessed won the prize. That sniper was a son of a bitch.

In the excitement, nobody noticed that Cole had worked his hands free. He held them behind his back, leaving the rope around his wrists. He kept his head down, not wanting to attract any attention to himself. He noticed that the South Korean was doing the same. If they'd shot an American POW just because he was wounded, then a South Korean POW was worth less than spit to these people.

He'd have to wait for the right moment, which wasn't going to be easy with that trigger-happy sniper. Besides, the odds were now down to six against four, with the six Chinese captors having weapons. It didn't look good. On the other hand, if Cole didn't make a move soon, they would be too far from the American line to ever get back.

The Chinese had their own timeline, but the deeper, drifted snow out here in the open was slowing them down. They kept shouting *Yídòng tā!* at their captives, their eyes glancing nervously at the clearing skies. Several planes prowled in the distance, mostly following the mountain ridges where it was likely that the main body of Chinese troops was hidden. Other planes flew cover for the American column, attacking enemy troops to clear a way for the Army retreat. These planes gave Cole a rough idea of where the road was located, although each step carried them farther away and closer to the Chinese headquarters. Overhead, the planes hovered and plunged like hawks over a field of newly mown hay. They circled in ever-widening loops, but never came close enough, although the sight of the planes was making the Chinese anxious.

At that moment, Cole got an idea. All they needed to do was get the attention of one of those planes. And he had a pretty good idea of how to do it. It was an idea that might also get him killed if it didn't go right. Then again, it was a given that the Chinese were going to kill them one way or another—either a slow death as POWs or quick like Thompson. Maybe it was better to get it over with quickly.

Finally, one of the planes broke free and flew an even wider pattern. This was too much for the Chinese, who shouted at their captives and pointed toward the nearest thicket. Apparently, the idea was to hide until the plane had gone past. Their Chinese captors seemed close to panic. Only the sniper managed to keep his cool, eying the plane warily, with his rifle raised partway to his shoulder, as if debating whether or not to shoot at it. The plane was coming at them from the west—the same direction as the lowering sun. So far, it didn't seem that the plane had spotted them because it hadn't changed altitude as it normally would for a bombing run or strafing. Not only that, but its path was going to take it west of their group, keeping closer to the distant road.

Fortunately for Cole, nobody was paying any attention to him. The Chinese had bigger problems now—one with two wings and a 500-pound payload that it was itching to drop on somebody's head.

Cole spoke quietly to Tommy nearby. "Kid, I want you to look right at the sun. See if you can get your glasses to flash at that plane."

He knew it was a long shot, but working in their favor was the fact that the pilot would be looking for anything on the ground that was out of the ordinary. A flash of sunlight off the lenses of the kid's glasses might be enough.

If they got lucky, the pilot of that Corsair was going to notice something glinting where there should only be rocks and brush. Cole held his breath. He was disappointed to see the plane start to move away.

But not for long. High above, the plane altered course and began to head right for them, dropping in altitude as it approached. Cole had seen it happen a dozen times before. The pilot was coming in for a strafing run, or maybe to drop a bomb. All those other times, however, Cole hadn't been on the receiving end. He had been a safe distance away, cheering on the pilot.

He had to admit that the sight of the plane coming directly at them was terrifying. One of the Chinese soldiers started firing at the plane, which only helped the pilot zero in on his target. The engines screamed as the plane began to dive.

Cole worked his hands free of the ropes and shouted, "Run!"

In an instant, the plane was upon them. The pilot gave them a burst that churned up the snow, sending captives and captors alike diving into the snowdrifts for cover. In the confusion, one of the Chinese soldiers dropped his rifle. Cole grabbed it.

The man shouted something at him and got hold of the rifle, but Cole wrenched the weapon from the man's grip, then hit him in the face with the rifle butt. Cole might have gotten shot by one of the others, but the plane was already circling back and coming in for another go at them. Those Corsairs were nimble. And this time, the pilot seemed to mean business. Cole just hoped to hell that he wasn't going to drop napalm. Cole didn't much like the idea of being turned into a burnt carcass.

Something fell from the plane, whistling as it came. Cole threw himself flat.

Seconds later, the explosion lifted him bodily into the air and tossed him several feet. Lucky for them, the pilot had overshot the target and the bomb had landed more than a hundred feet beyond them. Debris and snow filled the air. Somehow, Cole managed to hang onto the rifle.

He picked himself up and surveyed the damage. There was Pomeroy, more or less buried in the snow. The kid was picking himself up, none the worse for wear. Even the ROK soldier had managed to survive.

But so had at least some of the Chinese. Two were down, possibly stunned or wounded. But that left four enemy soldiers. One of them started to level his rifle at Cole, and Cole swung his own weapon in his direction and pulled the trigger, shooting from the hip, hoping to hell that the barrel wasn't completely clogged with snow.

The soldier fell. Pomeroy had freed his own hands by now—the rope wasn't all that tight—and had the sense to pick up the other rifle. The odds were getting better. But what the hell had happened to the Chinese sniper? He was the guy that Cole was worried about. The bomb had hit closer to that end of their single-file column, so maybe the sniper was buried in the snow by the blast—or even dead.

"Let's go!" Cole shouted. Nobody needed to say that twice. Cole and the others ran for it.

The deep snow made it hard to run with any sort of speed, so they were forced to follow the ruts they had made earlier. Pomeroy lurched wildly on his frostbitten feet. Cole couldn't even imagine how painful that must be. He turned and grabbed Pomeroy by his coat, dragging him. "Come on!"

A round passed over their heads with an angry crack and all three of them ducked. Cole spun and fired a couple of wild shots at the Chinese, not even bothering to aim. He just wanted to give them something to think about and maybe slow them down. Maybe they had gotten lucky and that bomb had taken out the Chinese sniper, who was the main opponent that Cole was worried about.

* * *

CHEN CAME TO SLOWLY. The last thing he remembered was the American plane bearing down on them, then the bomb falling from the sky. Everything had gone black after that.

He held himself very still, just listening. This was not easy because his ears rang. If the plane still hovered, he did not want to give them an excuse to attack again. It would be just like the Americans to waste a bomb on one man.

He couldn't hear it anymore. The plane seemed to have gone. Groaning, he slowly raised himself on one elbow, checking for damage. Snow clogged his nose and had gotten down the back of his coat. If that was the worst that had happened to him, then he was lucky. Then again, Chen always had been lucky. His luck included the fact that the bomb had fallen short, or he would be nothing more than a forgotten memory.

Slowly, he sat up, his head still ringing. He looked around. His rifle had fallen nearby in the snow and he reached for it, shaking off the snow. He gave the ugly wooden stock a quick inspection, and to his great relief, the rifle appeared fine. Whatever it lacked in beauty, the Mosin-Nagant was a sturdy weapon.

Next, he recalled that he had not been alone before the bomb fell from the sky. Where were the others? He saw the body of one of his comrades sprawled nearby, blood splashed bright against the snow. The contrast of colors was interesting to observe. For a moment, he became lost in contemplating that. He had seen an artist at work once, transferring bright paint to a blank canvas. The scene before him was much like that. He forced himself to focus.

Then he remembered. The prisoners! What had become of them? Everything began to come into sharper focus.

That's when he heard shots being fired, back in the direction where they had come from earlier.

Chen struggled to his feet and began to hurry in that direction.

CHAPTER TWENTY-FIVE

THE FOUR MEN hurried through the snow, Cole leading the way. Within minutes, they had reached the shallow ravine where the Chinese had captured them. So far, the Chinese were hanging back, content to take potshots at the Americans, wary of the fact that they were now armed.

But not armed with much. They only had the clips that had been in the rifles when they picked them up.

"Now what?" Pomeroy asked, breathing hard from slogging through the snow on his bad feet.

"We keep going," Cole said. "We'll follow our tracks all the way back to the road and catch up to the column."

"If they haven't left us behind," Pomeroy said.

"Let's hope to hell they haven't," Cole said. "How's your Chinese?"

"Very funny."

Looking on, Tommy and the South Korean looked too scared to talk. Cole had to wonder if the Korean even spoke English. "You're doing good," Cole said to them. He nodded reassuringly at the Korean soldier. "Stick with me and do what I say, and we'll get out of this mess."

"Whatever you say," Tommy said.

"All right then. Let's go."

There was no longer a path carved through the snow because their tracks were more spread out coming to this point. The good news was that the snow wasn't as deep, either, which made the going easier. The bad news was that following their original tracks was going to take longer to get back to the road. In the distance, Cole could see a couple more Corsairs flying back and forth, marking the location of the road. Heading out cross country toward the road rather than following their tracks would save them a lot of time.

It was a gamble, though. For all Cole knew, there might be a massive ravine in the way. Or more Chinese.

Beside him, Pomeroy saw Cole stop and came to a halt. He handed the rifle that he'd been carrying off to the kid and doubled over, hands on his knees.

"What are you thinking?" Pomeroy asked, panting.

"This way," he said.

They struck off to the southwest, the most direct route to catching up with the column. They ran up a hill and down the other side into a thicket of brush. Cole led the way, pushing through as branches and brambles snagged at his coat and pants. The branches that snapped off had a fresh, green smell that Cole found reassuring. Behind him, Pomeroy cursed. But Cole didn't mind the fact that the brush gave them some cover. He hadn't forgotten that the Chinese were still after them.

At that moment, a couple of rounds ripped through the brush. One of the bullets hit a trunk or maybe a rock and ricocheted with a spine-curdling twang. Cole ducked his head and kept going. He sensed that Pomeroy was slowing down as they continued to struggle through the brush.

Finally, they emerged on another slope with nothing more on it than the high-country grass pushing through a few inches of snow. The going was easier, but Cole didn't like the fact that they were exposed. The fact that the Chinese also had to push through the brush behind them was a slight reprieve, but that obstacle wouldn't last nearly long enough.

He raised the rifle and fired a couple of shots into the brush. He didn't have a prayer of hitting anything, but the Chinese wouldn't know that. The shots might make their pursuers slow down and use more caution.

Turning to the others he grunted, "Move your asses." However, he feared that the others were already going as fast as they could. Which wasn't going to be fast enough if they were going to have any hope of actually outrunning the enemy.

Up ahead, he saw yet more broken country that was going to slow them down. Damn, he thought to himself. Maybe that shortcut hadn't been the smartest thing to do.

But that's when he had an idea.

When they came to the ravine, he started down into it, leaving a good trail through the snow.

"OK, everybody stop," he said. "I want you to backtrack. Try to step in your old footprints, if you can."

"What the hell?" Pomeroy complained. "The last thing I need to do is run any more than I need to. We ought to just set an ambush and fight these bastards."

"With what, New Jersey? Snowballs? I've got maybe two shots left. What about the rifle the kid's got?"

"About the same," Tommy said.

"Four bullets ain't gonna take out five Chinese," Cole said. "We've got to outsmart them instead."

"Just how are we gonna do that?"

"Like this," Cole said. They had reached a kind of fork in the land-scape where the land had been wrenched apart by some long-ago glacier or earthquake. Part of the hill ran upward, while the rest ran down into the ravine from which they had just backtracked. The hill directly above them had a sloping, rocky surface that the wind had swept clean of snow. Nimbly, Cole jumped onto the bare rock, then turned to help the others climb up. From this point, they could run nearly a couple hundred feet across bare rock before reaching the crest of the hill.

"I get it now," Pomeroy said. He grinned at the thought that their tracks would run down into the ravine—and disappear. Meanwhile, they would be over the hill and out of sight—in nearly the opposite direction.

"We got to hoof it," Cole warned. "Can't let them see us."

"Go!" Pomeroy shouted, and surged ahead up the rocky slope, leading the way.

* * *

MINUTES LATER, Chen and the other Chinese emerged from the thicket, scratched and bleeding where the thorns had torn their bare skin. They had practically run through the thicket in their eagerness to recapture the escaped prisoners. While killing Americans was satisfying enough, bringing back actual prisoners to headquarters would have earned them accolades. Their officers had impressed upon them the fact that live prisoners would be worth a great deal as a bargaining chip, as long as they were not wounded. The Chinese had no interest in caring for enemy wounded because they were perceived as having less value.

With a note of bitterness, Chen noted how interesting it was that the Americans seemed to value the lives of their soldiers, while the Chinese military so eagerly tossed away the lives of its own troops. The Chinese would write off any captured troops rather than bargaining to get them back.

Chen was not really expecting an ambush, but they left the shelter of the thicket cautiously. To his relief, he saw the fleeing enemy's tracks heading away across the open ground. Still four men, running as a group.

"This way!" he shouted to the others. "Follow their tracks!"

He had quickly become the leader of this small squad. No one argued or offered to give up the chase. Like Chen, they knew the value of bringing back a prisoner. Who knew? Their reward might even be a bottle of rice wine. Such things did not much interest Chen, but he would welcome humiliating the enemy.

He thought about the American soldier with the strange eyes. Like a wolf's eyes, they had been. If nothing else, he at least had the man's knife now. Given half a chance, he was sure that the American would have killed him. Chen thought it was fortunate that most of the Americans he had seen were not hard men like that one.

Concentrate, he warned himself. Letting his thoughts wander was the surest way to get killed.

"Hurry!" he called to the others. "Keep your eyes open."

Here on the more open ground the snow was not as deep, most of it having blown into drifts that could be avoided. They trotted after the tracks, quickly covering the ground. Chen had to admit that he was enjoying the thrill of the chase, knowing that he had the upper hand. He was the hunter and the escaped prisoners were the quarry. It would not be long now.

They reached another ravine, and the tracks disappeared down into it. With any luck, they might find the escaped prisoners trying to climb out on the other side—some of these ravines were quite steep. They would be caught like rats.

He approached the ravine cautiously, just in case the enemy escapees were hiding there in an attempt at an ambush. They did have a couple of rifles, but Chen doubted that they had much ammunition.

Creeping up on the ravine, he saw with relief that the tracks led down. He waved the others on.

They clambered down to the rocky bottom of the ravine. Chen looked around for more tracks, but couldn't see any. The enemy soldiers had not simply disappeared. Aside from a couple of scraggly shrubs, there was not so much as a stick of cover for them to hide. Quickly, he searched the far side of the ravine and along its length for any sign of where the Americans had scrambled out, but there was nothing. The tracks had gone down into the ravine, but did not come back out.

"Where have they gone?" someone asked, peering around at the rocks as if the enemy had somehow crawled under them.

Slowly, it dawned on Chen that this was a trick. Cursing under his breath, he brought the others back up the slope to the top of the ravine. Panting from the effort, Chen and the others searched the ground, trying to figure out what had happened. It did not help that their own footsteps had already trampled the area. Whatever story the tracks in the snow had to tell was now badly muddled.

He looked around for some clue. There were no other tracks other than the ones leading to this spot. Nearby were large bare areas of rock that had been blown clean of snow by the incessant winter wind. Slowly, he realized that someone might just be able to jump onto those rocks and make his way toward the crest of the nearest hill without leaving any trace. The bare rocks stretched on for quite a distance, creating a blank slate. It would be impossible to tell which way their quarry had gone.

Chen began to realize that he had been thoroughly tricked.

The other men had come to the same conclusion. Sadly, they must have realized that their hopes for a bottle of rice wine had vanished. They now watched Chen expectantly, waiting for him to come up with a solution.

"Come on," he said, and led them up the hill. In this direction lay the entire American and U.N. column, creeping along the road. That was where the Americans had gone, and now that was where Chen and his squad were going, too.

* * *

COLE and the others covered as much ground as quickly as they could. They ran when they could and scurried across the broken and rocky places. Their legs and lungs protested in the high, cold mountain air, hearts hammering with exertion, but they pressed on.

"We've got to catch up to the column," Cole said. "If we get left behind, we're dead men."

Nobody argued. They knew as well as Cole did that this was their one and only chance of escaping the Chinese. If they missed the column and it had already moved on, they would be running right back into the arms of the enemy that was swarming in the column's wake. Even Pomeroy didn't bother to protest, but grimaced and ran on, despite the obvious pain in his frostbitten feet.

After half an hour, the road came into sight. They could see trucks moving on it and soldiers plodding beside the slow-moving vehicles. Cole had to admit that it wasn't an impressive sight. He was seeing a downtrodden, battered regiment, so different from the troops that had marched so rapidly toward the Yalu River just days before.

"Wave your hands so the dumb bastards don't think that we're Chinese and shoot us," Cole said.

Pomeroy and the others followed Cole's advice—several rifles had turned in their direction as they suddenly emerged from the landscape. Once the other soldiers had determined that they were not Chinese, thus posing no threat, their return to the column was largely ignored except for some idle curiosity.

"Where you boys been?" someone called.

"There's a burger joint just over that hill," Pomeroy replied. "Onion rings, too."

"Over that hill?" The soldier scoffed. "Nothin' over there but Chinese food."

The troops on the road had other things to worry about. To the rear of the column, a truck was blazing after being hit by grenades during a Chinese sneak attack. Flames shot from the tires and out of the windows, revealing the truck's metal skeleton. Cole hated to think about the poor wounded bastards who had been trapped inside.

Shots rang out. From above the column, enemy troops in the hills fired down sporadically at the American column. Occasionally, someone cried out and slumped over, hit by the random fire. There was no real cover from the shooting, so no one remarked on it or reacted much. The bullets were just an annoyance, like rain.

"This don't look good," Cole said. "We've still got a lot of miles to cover until Hagaru-ri. Hell, I'm beginning to wonder if there's even anybody left at Hagaru-ri. You'd think they'd send out some rein-forcements."

"This is a whole lot better than being captured," Pomeroy said. "But I got to say, it looks like we are out of the wok pan and into the wonton soup."

CHAPTER TWENTY-SIX

COLE COULD SEE that the entire column was falling apart. The unit had lost so many officers and non-commissioned officers that there were few left to direct the men and create any cohesion of purpose. They trudged along, mutual survival being the glue holding them together.

Sergeant Weber and Lieutenant Ballard did what they could to keep their own men going, but there was a lot of the column that was essentially leaderless.

"This is goddamn awful," Pomeroy muttered through gritted teeth. The escape from the Chinese had taken a lot out of him. It was clear that his feet pained him a great deal. Cole didn't want to think about what Pomeroy's feet looked like inside of those boots.

"How are them feet holding up? You want me to put you on one of the trucks?"

"Hell, no. Save the space for somebody who is actually wounded."

"Have it your way," Cole said. He wasn't going to argue. Targeted by the Chinese hit-and-run attacks, many of the trucks had become death traps for the wounded inside.

Upon returning to the column, they had discarded the unfamiliar Chinese rifles and re-armed themselves with American weapons. With so many wounded, there was no shortage of M-1 rifles and carbines. What they lacked was ammo.

Weber approached, holding a spare rifle. With surprise, Cole saw that it was a Springfield with a telescopic sight.

"You better take this," Weber said.

"Where did that come from?"

The sergeant shrugged. "Let's just say that the man who had it last won't be needing it." He handed Cole a handful of cartridges. "That is all we have. I know you will make each shot count. It is what a sniper does."

"Thanks, Sarge. You won't be disappointed."

Weber nodded curtly and walked off.

Cole hefted the rifle and admired how right it felt in his hands. It had been too long.

There would be time enough later to put the rifle to use. They were surrounded by enemy soldiers, after all. But first things first. There were more mundane things to deal with.

Cole changed his socks and made the kid do the same. His own toes had an ashen white look and felt waxen and numb, but they didn't seem to be frostbitten yet. He thought that it was a strange thing how with bullets and planes and mortars flying, the fight really came down to the state of a soldier's feet.

Progress had been agonizingly slow. First, the column had been halted by a major Chinese roadblock at Hill 1221. It had taken a coordinated attack led by the task force's commanding officer to push the Chinese off the high ground so that the column could get rolling once again.

Around them, the shadows in the hills began to deepen as night approached. Tangles of thickets covered the landscape, interspersed with boulders and ravines, offering perfect cover for the creeping enemy. As the sun sank lower, so did the temperature. They had worked up a sweat running from the Chinese, and now the damp clothing next to Cole's skin was starting to chill him. There wasn't time to change into anything dry.

He found a couple of overcoats and a slightly scorched blanket hanging off the back of a truck and grabbed them, giving one extra coat to the kid and draping the blanket across Pomeroy's shoulders. Pomeroy accepted the blanket without comment. The coat that he had grabbed for himself was far too big, like he was moving inside a tent, but in the falling temperatures he welcomed any added warmth that he could get.

"I've never seen anything like it," Pomeroy said.

"Me neither," Cole agreed. "Kid, you stick close with us, you hear?"

"I sure will," Tommy said. "One thing for sure is that I'm not going to go chasing off after any Chinese in the bushes again. It's a sure way to get captured."

Cole couldn't argue with that.

The South Korean soldier who had escaped with them also walked nearby, his own unit having scattered. Cole was glad to have the man around because he had shown a lot of fighting spirit. Cole caught his eye and nodded. They couldn't understand one another's words, but the message was clear enough. *I got your back and you got mine.*

The closest that Cole had witnessed to what was happening to the column was the Wehrmacht collapse at the Falaise Gap in 1944. But even then, the Germans' fierce discipline and spirit had somehow held their army together as it retreated back to Germany.

Looking around, Cole thought that this was something much worse. This was bad. This was the brink of annihilation. The thought had an unreal quality because this was not something that happened to the U.S. military.

He decided that this had nothing to do with courage. He had never seen such brave, tough men. But they were out of supplies. They had run out of food and medical supplies. Worst of all, the U.N. column was mostly out of ammunition. Trucks ran out of gas and had to be abandoned, sometimes with wounded still inside. The cries of injured men who knew they were being left behind were pitiful to hear.

It didn't help that the Chinese attacked relentlessly. Thank God that they couldn't seem to coordinate their attacks, but came at the column in squads—or maybe bunches—it was hard to make much sense of the Chinese forces, which still seemed largely disorganized. What mattered were that there were so damn many of them, and that they held the high ground. Uncontested, they flowed from peak to peak bordering the road, peppering the Americans with small arms fire, grenades, and even mortars on occasion. The Americans fired back, but soldiers were running out of ammunition up and down the column. For the enemy, this was turning into a goddamn turkey shoot.

To the rear, he heard a flurry of gunfire and shouting. It was too far back for him to join the fight without abandoning Pomeroy or the kid, which he wasn't eager to do. In the confusion and the growing darkness, he might never see them again. Cole looked and saw a fight taking place around a truck not more than one hundred feet away. He couldn't tell if it was the Americans pushing back the Chinese, or the Chinese overwhelming the truck's defenders. He got his answer when he heard a dull *whump* and saw a flare of orange flame as the truck was hit by a Chinese grenade.

This was awful. But it was about to get a whole lot worse.

Cole was just turning to say something to Pomeroy when a rifle cracked and a bullet plucked at his overcoat. Only the fact that the overcoat was a couple sizes too big saved Cole because the round passed through billowing fabric. Whoever had shot at him had not taken that into account.

Cole shoved Tommy down. Pomeroy and the South Korean were already scrambling for cover.

Deep within Cole, the Critter growled a warning. After all, Cole was nothing if not a creature of instinct. He sensed that the shot hadn't been random. Somebody out there had singled out their little group. Maybe even singled out *him*. Cole had a pretty good idea who it was—their old friend the Chinese sniper. The son of a bitch must have tracked them all the way back to the column. You had to give it to him for being persistent, that was for sure.

"Stay down," Cole hissed at the others. Keeping low, he charged for the cover offered by the nearest truck. Pomeroy followed, close on his heels.

* * *

CHEN HAD REACHED the retreating American column and saw with satisfaction that it was being cut to pieces. He was reminded of how, as a boy, he had once seen the family's chickens peck a snake to death. Attacked from all sides, the snake had exhausted itself striking blindly at the birds. Those hens had punished the snake in the process of killing it, just as the Chinese forces were now doing to the invaders.

There was no shortage of targets, but Chen did not immediately join the attack. He felt a sense of anger toward the captives who had escaped. They had caused him to lose face. The escapees might now think that they were safe, that they had outsmarted him, but he wanted to show them otherwise, which was why Chen was looking for them among the soldiers on the road.

He slipped along the edges of the column, moving like a wraith. He was sure that his quarry had rejoined the column in this vicinity. Now, it was just a matter of finding them among the confusion of troops and trucks.

Finally, he spotted the soldier with the markings on his helmet. Some sort of flag with crossed bars and stars. A rare smile creased Chen's face. The American was walking with a group of other men— very likely the same ones that he had escaped with. Chen had tracked them down.

Chen crept closer to the column, using caution. The Americans were in full retreat, but that did not mean they were not dangerous. When he reached the limits of the scrub brush that he was using for cover, he leveled the rifle at the soldier with the flag on his helmet. Chen considered a head shot, but decided against it as being too difficult. The target was moving, after all. Instead, he aimed for the larger target presented by the soldier's body and pulled the trigger.

To his disappointment, the soldier did not go down. Chen realized that perhaps he had become overconfident in his shooting skills. Even the best snipers missed from time to time. The soldier disappeared behind a truck while the band of men that he had been with scattered like rats.

Chen ran the bolt and loaded another round in the chamber. Where had the man gone? Finally, Chen saw the man's helmet appear from behind the truck and he settled his crosshairs on it. His finger began to take up tension on the trigger. Time to settle this business once and for all, he thought.

* * *

COLE HAD DUCKED behind the truck along with Pomeroy.

"I guess you pissed off that Chinese sniper," he said. "He came after you."

"What do you mean, I pissed him off? What about you?"

"You're the one who led the escape," Pomeroy pointed out. "Without you, we'd be locked up in some Chinese stockade by now."

"Thank you—I guess," Cole said. "It just figures that there is a whole war on, and this fella has to take it personal."

"What are you going to do about it?" Pomeroy asked. "You can't hide behind a truck forever."

"Take off your helmet," Cole said.

"What?"

"Here's what we're gonna do to draw him out. Take off your helmet and put it on the end of your rifle, then raise it above the hood of the truck, real slow."

"This actually works?"

"Sometimes," Cole said. "It's about fifty-fifty."

Pomeroy limped into position at the front of the truck and began to lift the helmet above the hood. If the driver of the truck thought that this was odd, he didn't say anything. Hell, he was probably too damn tired to notice.

Cole had positioned himself toward the back of the truck, keeping out of sight below the truck bed, off to one side of the back tire. He slipped off his gloves so that he could operate the rifle more effectively. He used the muddy tire itself to steady the rifle.

He knew that Pomeroy had carried out his assignment when he saw the muzzle flash of the enemy sniper's rifle in the gathering gloom beyond the edge of the road. The Chinese sniper had taken the bait.

Cole fired as soon as he saw the muzzle flash. He strained his eyes to see, but was not able to make out any sort of actual target. This was all guesswork. The flash in the dark was the best that he could hope for here.

He ran the bolt and fired again in the same general direction. Though low on ammo, just maybe he would get lucky. When there was no returning fire, Cole thought maybe that was the case. Maybe he had nailed that sniper, after all. Deep inside him, the Critter was less convinced. He felt his warning instincts stir uneasily. Cole kept searching, but couldn't make out any targets in the gathering gloom.

If that Chinese sniper wasn't dead, then where the hell had he gone?

* * *

COLE CREPT around the sheltered side of the truck and found Pomeroy eyeing a hole in his helmet.

"I'll tell you one thing," Cole said. "That Chinese feller can shoot."

"Be glad that wasn't on your actual head."

"Did you get him?"

"Maybe, maybe not. Stick your head out and see."

"No thanks. I'm good right here."

The column still hadn't moved. Up ahead, they could hear intense firing as some sort of battle got going. Word was coming back that the Chinese had put up a roadblock at a hairpin turn in the road to Hagaru-ri. There was no way around it because of the steep terrain. The only way was to go forward by fighting their way through the enemy roadblock, which wasn't proving easy. Not only were the Americans and their allies exhausted, freezing cold, and low on ammo, but there had already been a terrible price to pay in trying to remove the roadblock.

"Did you hear?" somebody said. "The lieutenant colonel has been hit. Doesn't look good. Who the hell's in charge now, anyhow?"

First the colonel, then the second-in-command who had gotten them to this point. Both brave and highly capable men. So many other lower-ranking officers had met the same fate. It was hard to say whether the Chinese had targeted the officers, or if they had simply been more exposed to enemy fire due to their leadership efforts. With so many of the officers taken out, it was starting to become a situation where it was every man for himself. Cole didn't like it, not one bit. He didn't always like officers or agree with them, but a unit as a whole needed leadership to hold it together.

With the column stalled by the roadblock and no clear plan of action evident, the enemy grew emboldened. More heavy firing tore into the column from the surrounding hills. Up and down the column, Chinese squads carried out hit and run attacks, brutally targeting the trucks loaded with wounded or supplies. The enemy was being drawn to the stalled soldiers like moths to a sputtering flame. As darkness fell, the situation grew more desperate.

The lieutenant came along, Sergeant Weber following in his wake. Since Cole didn't smoke anymore, Pomeroy bummed a cigarette off the sergeant.

"What's the matter, Sarge, you didn't get enough fighting in the last war?" Pomeroy asked Weber.

The German shrugged. "Being a soldier was all I knew. When I came to America, it was the only job I could get."

"Huh. You think the Wehrmacht would be in this jam?"

"You ever hear of Russia, my friend?"

The lieutenant signaled for the nearest men to gather around.

"Listen, fellas. I'm going to be honest with you. The situation is not good. The road ahead is good and plugged tighter than the cork in my grandma's whiskey jug. We've tried to push the Chinese off, but no go. We just don't have the men or the ammo."

It was shocking to hear that they were now cut off from Hagaru-ri. The men listening absorbed the information stoically.

"What are your orders, sir?" asked a soldier who looked a decade older than the lieutenant.

"We all know that this road leads south to Hagaru-ri," he said. "What we don't know is whether or not we still *hold* Hagaru-ri. The base may have been overrun. We just don't know, but it's the only chance we've got. The thing is, there's another way to get there besides the road. Basically, the lake runs parallel to the road. If you get out there on the ice and head south, you'll reach our guys—if they're still there."

"Are you saying we ought to make a run for it? What about the wounded? We can't just leave them."

"Listen, I am not saying it's every man for himself. Stick together. I'm going to take one of these trucks and try to get it across the ice. I don't even know if there's enough gas for that, but I'm sure going to try."

The lieutenant moved away toward the nearest truck, and a group of men gathered around him—not more than twenty. It suddenly became clear that this was all the direction that they were going to get. The lieutenant had claimed that it wasn't every man for himself—but he was wrong about that. Surrounded and trapped, the task force soldiers now had to survive any way that they could. The unit was splintering.

Knowing that he had come to a crossroads of sorts, Cole considered his options. He always had been a loner, since his earliest days hunting and trapping in the mountains back home. He knew that his own chances of survival were likely better if he struck out on his own. Alone, he could easily dodge the Chinese and reach the American lines —wherever they were. His best option was to go it alone.

He looked around at the other faces nearby: Pomeroy, the kid, and half a dozen others he barely knew. They looked scared but determined. No way in hell would he ever leave them alone.

Cole nodded at another truck. "You heard the lieutenant. Let's grab that truck and get as many of those wounded out of here as we can."

CHAPTER TWENTY-SEVEN

"LET'S MOVE OUT," Cole said. "Leave anything you can't carry."

"What about my rifle?" Tommy asked, stammering. Cole wasn't sure if the kid was cold, or scared, or maybe a little of both. *Can't blame him none on either count*, Cole thought.

"Leave everything *except* your rifle," Cole clarified. "There may be Chinese between here and where we want to be."

The driver of the truck was a young soldier named Kelwick. Improbably, he was chewing gum and blowing bubbles in the bitter cold. He also was riding up front alone, which was unusual. "Ain't you got a passenger?" Cole asked.

"He died," Kelwick said, pointing to a bullet hole in the windshield. It wasn't any secret that the Chinese were targeting the truck drivers as a way to knock out the vehicles. Whatever else he was, Kelwick was a brave son of a bitch.

"You up for this?" Cole asked him.

"Not much choice there, buddy," Kelwick said. "It's either drive out onto that ice or stay here for the Chicoms."

Cole nodded. "Pomeroy, you better ride shotgun."

"I can walk."

He had figured that Pomeroy would argue about riding in the

truck. "Save your energy, New Jersey. You might need it. Get in the damn truck. Kelwick, how are you fixed for fuel?"

"I've got enough gas for maybe five or six miles," he said. "How far do you think we've got to go?"

"That might be enough gas, but who the hell knows. See what I mean, Pomeroy? Better save your energy. You might have to walk the rest of the way, after all."

The cabin of the truck was cramped and uncomfortable, but at least Pomeroy could get some of the weight off his feet.

All along the road, similar scenes were taking place. The few officers who were left tried to maintain order and lead as many men as they could to safety—or what they hoped was safety, because it was not a given that they would be fleeing into the arms of the Marines rather than the Chinese. So much uncertainly gave every action a tang of fear.

However, it was more of a certainty that to be left behind in one of the trucks meant death—the Chinese didn't seem all that interested in taking any of the wounded as prisoners. They didn't want to be bothered caring for them.

By way of proof, they had to look no further than the rear of the column, where several trucks burned. The crackling flames could not entirely cover up the screams of the wounded men being burned alive, unable to get out of the trucks before they had been hit by grenades, mortars, or machine-gun fire. Now that it was growing dark, the flames reflected off the snow-covered hills, illuminating the landscape in a flickering glare like some frozen hellish scene. Visible from time to time were the quilted uniforms of the Chinese, creeping ever closer. Cole wrinkled his nose at the awful smell of burning gasoline and rubber tires, mixed with the telltale smell of burning human flesh. Having experienced that in Europe, it was a smell that he had hoped never to experience again.

"Here we go!" Kelwick shouted, blowing one last bubble for good measure.

The truck bumped wildly as it left the road and headed down the gentle slope toward the frozen reservoir. Inside, the wounded men held on for dear life, becoming even more battered in the process. Bad as this ride was turning out to be, it was much better than being left behind for the Chinese.

A handful of soldiers walked beside the truck, pausing now and then to help push it out of a hole. Exhausted, hungry, and mostly frozen, they kept their weapons at the ready.

The reservoir itself was shaped a bit like a crow's foot. They were headed onto the lower right-hand prong that led toward Hagaru-ri— and hopefully toward help. Not that the soldiers would have known or cared, but this was a man-made lake and its Korean name was the Changjin Lake. *Chosin* was the Japanese pronunciation, remaining from when the imperialist Japanese had occupied Korea and used it as a hunting ground for the Siberian tigers, bears, leopards, and wolves that had once roamed the mountains. Those predators had been hunted to extinction by Japanese big game hunters in the early 1900s, but plenty of dangerous two-legged predators now roamed the landscape.

Finally, the truck gave one last, tremendous lurch and drove out onto the ice itself. The change from the rocky ground to the smooth ice was jarringly abrupt. It was almost eerie, the sudden switch to flat terrain after days of staring at nothing but hills, ravines, and mountains.

"Keep your eyes open," Cole warned them. "We don't know what's in front of us, and we sure as hell know that the Chinese are right behind us. Kelwick, you know where you're headed?"

"Easy, peasy," he said, popping his gum. "All I have to do is head south and keep it between the mountains. Just like Route 1. I ought to be able to do that."

Kelwick wasn't exaggerating. The surface of the frozen lake stretched before them, about a mile wide. Hills and mountains ringed the rest of the lake. All that Kelwick had to do was stay on the ice.

Visibility was less than perfect due to the blowing snow, however, and crossing the ice posed its own obstacles. The biggest challenge was avoiding the drifts. Although it hadn't snowed today, the cold, dry snow still continued to blow around. The snow was more than a foot deep in places, drifting even deeper in others. Here and there, the ice had been impacted by stray bombs or artillery rounds, leaving craters. If Kelwick didn't want to get stuck, he would have to avoid these.

Although it was full dark by now, a kind of glow reflected off the snow-covered ice and lighted their way. The driver didn't dare turn on his headlights, thus making the truck a target, so the glow was welcome. No moon or stars showed, so the sky overhead must have had cloud cover. Cole hoped it wasn't going to snow any damn more—he'd had enough of that. He sniffed the air and didn't think that it smelled like snow, though.

Here and there in the distance, he saw other vague shapes on the ice as small groups like their own made a run for it. At least, Cole hoped that these were more of their own troops. For all he knew, these might be Chinese coming after them.

Seeing the American and UN forces retreat wasn't enough for them, apparently. They wanted to see their enemy destroyed.

"Let's go," Cole said. "Get moving. And keep an eye open for what's ahead. The last thing we want to do is surprise our own boys and get machine-gunned."

Kelwick nodded and kept the window rolled down despite the cold, in order to communicate with the soldiers around him.

The wind blew even harder out here, flowing down from the mountains with added velocity. Loose snow swirled, occasionally reducing the visibility ahead to a few feet.

Cole did not particularly like being in the open. He preferred having trees and mountains around. Out here, they were sitting ducks if the enemy appeared.

But at the moment, there were more immediate concerns.

"Can't see a damn thing!" Kelwick shouted.

"Just go," Cole said. "Keep driving."

The truck crept along in low gear. Cole gritted his teeth against the icy crystals rubbing his face. They had come this far, and they had to keep going. Rescue might be just a few miles away, but it was going to be one hell of a trek.

Behind them, from the section of lake shore that they had left from, he heard the sound of a horn. He took a few steps away from the truck so that he could better hear the sound. He thought that maybe his ears were playing tricks on him. Not a truck horn, he decided, but a bugle. Then he heard it again.

"You hear that?" Tommy asked. "It's that bugle sound we heard the nights we were attacked."

"It's the Chinese," Cole said. "They're letting us know that they're coming after us."

"What should we do, Cole?" the kid sounded near panic, fear and exhaustion plain in his voice.

"Keep moving." Cole raised his voice. "Everybody, get a move on."

At the wheel, Kelwick eased into a slightly higher gear. However, he couldn't go much faster if the men on foot had any hope of keeping up. This wasn't going to be fast enough. Behind them, they heard another bugle, closer this time.

Kelwick stopped the truck. "Everybody get on," he shouted. With the wounded taking up the back, it wasn't clear where the men on foot were supposed to ride. A rifle fired behind them, then another. Rounds cracked overhead. The Chinese were getting closer. "Get on the hood, if you have to. We've got to *move*."

The men were so stiff with cold that climbing onto the truck was easier said than done. Three men wedged themselves into the back, hanging on for dear life. Cole and Tommy got in front, barely squeezing in. In fact, the kid was basically sitting in Cole's lap. With an effort, Cole was able to pull the door shut.

"Everyone on?" Kelwick shouted out the open window, his foot bouncing on the clutch so that the truck rocked back and forth.

In answer, somebody slapped the side of the truck twice. Good to go.

A bullet passed overhead. "Move it," Cole said.

Kelwick let out the clutch, shifting from first to second to third. It was the first time in weeks that he'd been able to drive at any kind of speed. The roads had been too rough for that. The frozen surface of the reservoir was snowy, but at least it was smooth.

The problem was visibility. Without headlights, it was hard to see more than a few feet ahead. Snow swirled in the gusts off the mountains, creating white-out conditions that Kelwick had no choice but to plunge through blindly. He couldn't slow down every time that the wind blew. He leaned forward over the bucking steering wheel, his nose practically touching the windshield, straining to see.

They didn't get far. With a tremendous jolt, the front passenger tire suddenly dropped into a hole.

"Hang on!" Kelwick shouted as he wrestled with the wheel.

The rest of the truck slewed around, tires skidding on the ice. The momentum tipped the truck over as if in slow motion. Even over the noise of the brakes and tires protesting, they could hear the muffled cries of the men in back. Finally, the truck came to rest tilted mostly onto its passenger side. The truck creaked and groaned ominously, as if it might not be finished with his plan to roll onto its side.

"What the hell did we hit?"

Cole couldn't get the door open easily to inspect the damage because it was pinned by the weight of the truck. He shoved it hard, and finally wriggled out, which wasn't easy in the over-sized greatcoat.

Immediately, he saw the problem. A massive hole yawned in the ice at his feet, and Cole instinctively took a step back before it swallowed him. He guessed that the hole had likely been caused by a stray bomb or artillery shell. In the dark and blowing snow, it would have been impossible for the driver to detect. The front tire had gone into the hole with such force that it now appeared bent. Tiny snorts of steam escaped from the front grill and were whisked away in the cold breeze.

A round passed over his head from the darkness leading to the lake shore, causing him to duck.

Two things became clear to him at once. First, the Chinese were catching up. Second, the truck wasn't going anywhere. Their only choice now would be crossing the ice on foot. How they were going to stay ahead of their pursuers when there were so many wounded to carry had yet to be seen—but Cole had an idea.

Kelwick had climbed out of the precariously leaning truck to inspect the damage, and quickly came to the same conclusion that Cole had.

"She's done in," he said. He snapped his bubble gum for emphasis.

"We need to get everybody out," Cole said. "Pomeroy! Kid! Let's go! Get out of the truck now! We've got to hoof it."

Kelwick leaned in close and spoke in a low voice. "The Chinese are right behind us. We could leave the wounded. We might have a shot of staying ahead of them, then."

"Hell no, we ain't leaving the wounded."

Cole said it with such vitriol that Kelwick stepped back. "Hey, it was just an idea. Forget I mentioned it."

Cole turned away and began helping Pomeroy and Tommy get the wounded from the back of the truck. There proved to be a dozen men riding in back. Half of them could walk, if just barely—but they would have to if they hoped to escape the Chinese. There turned out to be just five men to carry on stretchers. The sixth man was dead, his body already stiff with cold. Nobody knew what else to do with him, so they left his body beside the truck, laying it down gently.

They divided the stretchers among the men who weren't wounded —at least not seriously. Tommy and New Jersey took one of the stretchers between them. Cole shook his head, seeing the way that Pomeroy was limping.

"You ought to be the one on that goddamn stretcher, New Jersey."

"Aw, stuff it, Hillbilly. Why don't you help, then?"

"I've got other things to do." Cole raised his voice. "Who here has got a grenade?"

One of the other soldiers gave him a grenade. Surprisingly, Kelwick had an entire magazine in his carbine, which he handed to Cole. "Have at it," he said. "I never was much of a shot."

"All right, here's the plan," Cole said. "Head south across the ice, straight down the lake. You ought to hit Hagaru-ri in an hour. Pomeroy here is in charge. Do what he says and you'll be all right."

"What the hell are you going to do?" Pomeroy demanded.

"I'm going to hold them up," he said.

"Like hell you are."

"Don't worry," Cole said. "I'll catch up."

Looking around at their faces, it was clear that none of them believed him. Hell, Cole himself didn't really believe it. "Go on now," he said. "That's an order."

"What, are you a general now, too?" Pomeroy demanded. "Come with us. You can't possibly stop those Chinese."

"One good man with a rifle is all it takes to make a difference," Cole said. "Tonight, you'll have to make do with me. Now, get going."

The others didn't need to be told twice. They set off across the ice, although it wasn't easy going for the wounded or for those carrying stretchers. Everyone was already beyond exhaustion, but they either had to somehow keep going, or sit down in the snow to die. Not much of a choice, was it?

Only Pomeroy and the kid lingered, as if waiting for Cole to change his mind. Finally, Pomeroy muttered a curse and struck out into the night. He and the kid, bearing the stretcher between them, were swallowed up by the darkness and the swirling snow.

Cole was left alone at the wreckage of the truck. From the darkness, he could hear the shouts of the pursuing Chinese and an occasional shot—what they were shooting at he had no idea because the visibility was so limited. But soon enough, they would come within sight of the wreck. Quickly, Cole assessed his defensive position. This wrecked truck was going to be his Alamo.

But he wasn't entirely alone.

He took hold of the dead man and dragged him around to the front of the truck. It was a gruesome task, and he hated to mess with a dead man as much as anyone else, but this soldier had one last duty even in death.

The steel truck frame offered plenty of cover. Cole got down low and stretched the body out on the ice beside the driver-side truck tire that wasn't in the hole. One of the wounded men had left behind his empty rifle, and Cole got it now and wedged it in the soldier's dead limbs so that it looked as if the dead man was firing the weapon.

Then Cole got in position and waited. He had Kelwick's carbine and his own Springfield with two rounds. The Chinese had fallen quiet, which spooked Cole. He just hoped that it meant they were creeping closer.

He wasn't disappointed. A shot cracked out, pinging off the metal truck. Then another. Cole squinted into the darkness. The first Chinese soldier took form almost like a ghost, grayish white in his quilted uniform, rifle at the ready. Cole put his sights on him and fired.

Another soldier appeared, dropping to his knee and firing in the direction of Cole's muzzle flash. Cole took him out. More shapes appeared. He picked another target and fired. Two bullets left. Not nearly enough. He fired twice more, and the weapon was empty. He tossed aside the carbine and picked up the more familiar Springfield rifle.

Cole's shooting had convinced the Chinese to halt their attack. There did not seem to be a large number of them. But there were more than two, which meant that Cole was in trouble.

The Chinese had no cover and were disadvantaged because he could just begin to see their silhouettes against the whiteness of the ice in between gusts of windblown snow, whereas Cole had the truck and the darkness.

That changed when one of the Chinese pitched a phosphorous grenade into the night, lighting up the scene on the ice. It was likely that the grenade had been scavenged from what was left of the convoy —the Americans' own weapons were being turned against them by the enemy.

If they could see *him*, he could also see *them*—but with just two shots left, it wasn't going to do him much good. He squeezed off a shot and took out the soldier who had thrown the grenade before he got any other bright ideas.

In the glaring light, he counted ten Chinese soldiers advancing. In their own way, they were as tough and heroic as the American soldiers. Cole would give them that much.

They were also awfully close. To his surprise, he saw that one was carrying a sniper rifle. The light wasn't good enough for Cole to see his face, but Cole had no doubt that this was the same soldier who had tracked him earlier today. How many Chinese snipers could there be? This guy was persistent.

With the whole scene lit up by the burning phosphorous, the Chinese sniper also spotted Cole and raised his rifle. Cole got his sights on the guy at just the same time. But the Chinese sniper was *fast*. A bullet thwacked into the tire next to Cole's head.

Cole's finger twitched as his last bullet left the rifle. He saw the enemy sniper snatch at one side of his head. By some miracle, had Cole hit him?

He might never know, because the phosphorous grenade began to fizzle out. But his last glimpse before the lights went out had been of the enemy slowly advancing. They weren't rushing him. Of course, they couldn't know that Cole was out of ammunition.

He had one final surprise planned for them.

Cole reached for the grenade and pulled the pin, then wedged the grenade under the dead soldier's frozen body beside him. It was a little tricky getting the positioning right to keep the handle squashed down, because if he messed this up he'd be saving the Chinese some trouble. But the solid weight was enough to hold the handle in place.

He heard snow crunch under a boot. They were *right there*. Quickly, he put his helmet with the Rebel flag on the dead man's head. Then Cole rolled to his feet and ran for all he was worth.

He was still running, flat out, when the grenade went off thirty seconds later. It could only mean that someone had gotten curious and rolled over what they thought was his body back at the truck.

Cole allowed himself a small grin, but he didn't stop running.

CHAPTER TWENTY-EIGHT

AN HOUR LATER, a Marine sentry thought that his eyes were playing tricks on him when he saw a figure emerging from the swirling, wind-blown snow on the ice. The pale background of snow-covered ice revealed the silhouette of a man approaching steadily. How anyone could survive that freezer blast of Mongolian winter scouring the ice was more than he could understand.

Was it the enemy? He had yet to see any Chinese, but he knew they were out there. He raised his weapon, itching to pull the trigger.

But he didn't shoot. Survivors from the disastrous Army column had wandered in off the lake for hours, but that had slowed to a trickle, then stopped. He was sure that the next soldier he saw was going to be speaking Chinese.

"Halt!" he shouted, struggling to make himself heard over the sounds of wind and sifting snow. His voice was swallowed up and lost. The silhouette advanced rapidly. He shouted a little louder: "Halt!"

"Point that somewhere else before you hurt yourself," the approaching soldier shouted back with a distinctive twang. "Goddamn trigger-happy leathernecks."

The sentry finally lowered his rifle. Up close, he could see that this was a real, live American. Snow covered his uniform and dusted his eyelashes and eyebrows above the scarf that covered the man's face. The eyes glittered like ice.

"You're from the task force?" the Marine asked.

"No, I'm going door to door selling Bibles. You want one?"

The Marine grinned. "Got one already. Hell, I thought you might be the Chinese."

Cole shook his head. "There was some Chinese back there, but I don't reckon there's enough of them left now to fill a bucket. Grenade," he added by way of explanation.

"Huh."

"Then again, keep your eyes open. They are determined sons of bitches. Now, where the hell can I find the aid station?"

The sentry looked him up and down in surprise. The loping figure had not seemed to be injured. "You wounded?"

"No, but my buddies are. They came in off the ice maybe an hour ago."

The Marine pointed. "Thataway."

Cole walked in that direction, passing more and more Marines, plus a few machine-gun emplacements, which was reassuring. If the Chinese did appear, that would chew them up but good. He wouldn't mind returning the favor, after all. He didn't like to admit it, but the enemy had turned the Army column into chow mein.

There had simply been too many of the enemy and the soldiers had been short on everything: decent food, ammo, gasoline, any chance of getting warm or medical aid, and ultimately leadership due to the death of so many good officers. It was no fault of the higher-ranking officers, he thought. They simply hadn't survived, but had given their lives for their country.

* * *

COLE AND THE OTHER SOLDIERS, as well as the Marines, had basic needs on their minds. But there were much larger forces already at work as the survivors trickled in across the ice.

If General Almond's push to the Yalu River had succeeded without Chinese intervention, then the Korean War might have indeed been won by Christmas and the soldiers of Task Force Faith would have been heroes, just as much as everyone else. Instead, massive numbers of Chinese troops had shown that victory in war is never as much of a certainty as it seems.

General Almond would have been hailed as another Patton, instead of a Custer.

For the soldiers of what came to be known as Task Force Faith after the fearless lieutenant colonel who had led the effort, there would be no storybook ending and precious little recognition. Soon, the loss of the Army contingent would be trumpeted as a defeat. The Marines who had survived the Chosin Reservoir would receive medals, but not the Army soldiers. For them, there would be only ignominy. Somebody needed a scapegoat to blame for the Chosin Reservoir.

Mostly, it was politics and public relations at play. Newspapers across the United States had closely followed the Chosin Reservoir campaign on their front pages. The looming encirclement and defeat had been trumpeted in bold headlines.

The censorship that had filtered much of the news during WWII was not present in 1950 for various reasons, so that American audiences were getting something much closer to the unvarnished truth about the war in Korea. The news that came home was of a cold, ragged, ill-equipped, frostbitten, and utterly defeated military in the face of overwhelming numbers of mostly Chinese troops.

For whatever reason, it was the story of the Marines that captured the public attention when General O.P. Smith had famously declared that his men were not retreating from the Chosin Reservoir, but were, "Fighting in a different direction." That was the spirit that the American public preferred to embrace when it came to the Korean War.

It didn't help that the United States government was looking for heroes during a difficult war in Korea. It also didn't help that the military and the public still lived in the shadow of the legacy of the Second World War, when the U.S. forces had always fought an offensive battle, gobbling up territory as fast as the enemy could retreat.

Now, the tables had turned. Never mind the fact that the soldiers had endured beyond any reasonable limits or expectations. The U.S.

military and government preferred to look the other way when it came to Task Force Faith.

The butcher's bill was heavy. More than a thousand Americans died in the fight or after being captured by the Chinese. Hundreds more South Koreans also gave their lives for their country. For hundreds more, their war was now over due to frostbite or battle wounds. The Chinese toll was staggering, with as many as ten thousand dead—possibly half of whom had simply frozen to death.

In suffering, all men are equal.

* * *

NONE of that mattered now to Cole. He and the survivors would have years to chew the gristle of the Chosin Reservoir campaign. He just wanted to see if Pomeroy was all right, and wherever Pomeroy was, he was sure that the kid would be nearby.

He walked on until he found the aid station. He pulled aside the canvas flaps and was greeted by a gust of warmth. That was welcome. Much less welcome were the field hospital smells that assaulted his nose—rubbing alcohol, disinfectant, blood, unwashed bodies, and a whiff of fecal smell. Smelled something like a slaughterhouse, if truth be told. His nose wrinkled.

Outside the tent walls, generators labored in the cold. Lights had been set up, just enough for the medical staff to navigate by. The medics were doing what they could to help the wounded troops.

In the confusion, there didn't seem to be much order or anyone to ask for help finding Pomeroy, so Cole had to wander the rows of men. Most of them lay on the frozen ground. Cole tried not to look too closely at some of the injuries. It was a wonder that some of these poor boys still lived. The question was, would they even make it to morning?

The relative warmth made Cole's cheeks and ears sting as they thawed, but he didn't think he had frostbite. Having spent his boyhood trapping and hunting in the mountains, he was no stranger to what it meant to be cold. Even his feet felt as if they were in good shape, which was more than he could say for the dozens of poor bastards whose heavily bandaged extremities spoke of fingers and toes lost to the cold.

Almost guiltily, what did register was how hungry he felt. When was the last time he had eaten anything?

Finally, he caught a glimpse of a kid with glasses and recognized Tommy Wilson, sitting on the ground beside a wounded man. Cole was momentarily taken aback at the sight of the kid because he hadn't seen him in weeks without his helmet off. His hair had grown during that time, and now Tommy's blondish hair looked jarring and out of place. Peach fuzz covered his face.

"I'll be damned," he said, walking up to them. "Look at you, all growed up."

Cole shook his head at the realization that the kid was barely old enough to shave, but had survived combat. Didn't seem right, in some ways.

Tommy lurched to his feet and Cole had to steady him. "You made it! I never thought we'd see you again."

"I said that I would catch up, didn't I?" He looked down at Pomeroy, who opened his eyes long enough to mutter, "You damn hillbilly." He then drifted off back to sleep.

"They've got him dosed up," the kid explained.

"How's he doing?"

"A lot better than most," the kid said quietly. "I was here when they took his boots off. It was—" Tommy struggled for a word, blanched at the memory.

"Bad," Cole said.

"Yeah, it was bad. With any luck, he'll be on a plane to Japan soon, where there's an actual hospital."

Cole bent down and tugged Pomeroy's blanket up to his chin, then patted the sleeping man's shoulder. The blanket did not quite cover Pomeroy's heavily bandaged feet. Looking at those feet, Cole wondered how it was possible that the man had somehow stayed upright for so many miles. Sheer willpower. Looking around at the similarly bandaged men, he could see that Pomeroy hadn't been the only man so determined to keep going.

Cole wasn't much for emotion, but he felt a lump in his throat.

Look at all these ugly bastards, he thought. *Every last one of them deserves a medal.*

He straightened up and asked the kid, "You hungry?"

"You kiddin' me? I could eat a horse."

"Be careful what you wish for, kid. There's no telling what they're serving up in the mess tent. Anyhow, let's take our chances and go find some grub."

If the medics in the aid station were doing the best they could for the wounded, the mess staff was no less heroic. Tents had been set up, and while they were not as warm as the hospital tents, they did keep the wind off and they smelled a whole lot better.

Supplies remained limited, but the emphasis was on hot grub. That meant gallons of strong coffee. Pancakes and syrup. Pots of soup that was mostly salty broth with some potatoes in it, but served piping hot. Cole and Tommy loaded up on all of it and then sat down on a couple of wooden boxes to eat. There weren't any tables, but there were a few familiar faces. He spotted Sergeant Weber, who gave him a nod, locking eyes with him for a moment. Coming from the gruff German, it was a sign of respect.

Drinking coffee nearby was Kelwick, the driver from the truck. He did a double-take when he spotted Cole. "I've got to say that I never thought I'd set eyes on you again. Not living, anyhow. What happened?"

"I held them off as long as I could, and then I got the hell out of there."

"We never would have made it if you hadn't bought us that time," Kelwick said. He flexed his arms and shoulders. "That was one hell of a long way to carry a stretcher. They'll fly more of the wounded out at daylight, your buddy with them. They're posting guards at the planes on account of guys trying to get out who aren't wounded."

"Trying to get out of Dodge," Cole said. "Can't say I blame them. But the fight ain't over."

"Yep. Eat some chow, get some sleep. The war starts again tomorrow, unless the Chinese decide to attack tonight."

Cole shook his head. "They've got to be just as cold and hungry as we are, if not worse. But they keep on coming."

"Yeah," Kelwick agreed. "So much for being home by Christmas. That sure as hell isn't happening now."

Had it really been just a few days ago that so many soldiers had actually thought that the war was almost over? The drive to the Yalu River had promised to end the conflict. He shook his head, musing that generals were a bunch of fools. It always fell on the troops in the field to sort things out.

Cole ate his fill, surprising himself by how much he ate, but was truly amazed by the number of pancakes that Tommy put away. Did that kid have a hollow leg, or what?

Finished, they walked out into the night, looking for a place to sleep. Cole stood for a while, his eyes adjusting to the darkness, surveying the surrounding hills and mountains that were just visible in the starlight reflected by the snowy peaks. He had a feeling that he was about to get to know these mountains a whole lot better. Somewhere up there, an untold number of Chinese and ROK troops were bedded down. Even now, they might be looking down at *him*.

"Come on, kid," he said, nodding toward a shelter that had been rigged against the wind. They could just squeeze in there for the night.

Like Kelwick had said, the war started again tomorrow.

-End-

NOTE TO READERS

It is hard to imagine the difficulties faced by the troops who fought at the Chosin Reservoir that bitter year of 1950. Their sacrifices helped lead to the free nation of South Korea today. Please note that the order of some events in this book has been changed somewhat to better suit the story.

Of course, this is a fictionalized account of events. For a good overview of the Korean War, consider *The Korean War* by Max Hastings or watch the documentary film, *Task Force Faith*, directed by Julie Precious. Thank you for reading, and to those who served in Korea, we are forever grateful.

— D.H.

ABOUT THE AUTHOR

David Healey lives in Maryland where he worked as a journalist for more than twenty years. He is a member of the International Thriller Writers and a contributing editor to The Big Thrill magazine. Visit him online at:

www.davidhealeyauthor.com
or
www.facebook.com/david.healey.books

Thank you for reading! If you enjoyed the story, please consider leaving a review on Amazon.com.

f